EDGE OF EON

EON WARRIORS #1

ANNA HACKETT

Edge of Eon

Published by Anna Hackett

Copyright 2018 by Anna Hackett

Cover by Melody Simmons of BookCoversCre8tive

Edits by Tanya Saari

ISBN (ebook): 978-1-925539-62-2

ISBN (paperback): 978-1-925539-63-9

This book is a work of fiction. All names, characters, places and incidents are either the product of the author's imagination or are used fictitiously. Any resemblance to actual persons, events or places is coincidental. No part of this book may be reproduced, scanned, or distributed in any printed or electronic form.

WHAT READERS ARE SAYING ABOUT ANNA'S ACTION ROMANCE

Unexplored – Romantic Book of the Year (Ruby) Novella Winner 2017

Unfathomed and Unmapped - Romantic Book of the Year (Ruby) finalists 2018

At Star's End – One of Library Journal's Best E-Original Romances for 2014

Return to Dark Earth – One of Library Journal's Best E-Original Books for 2015 and two-time SFR Galaxy Awards winner

The Phoenix Adventures – SFR Galaxy Award Winner for Most Fun New Series and "Why Isn't This a Movie?" Series

Beneath a Trojan Moon – SFR Galaxy Award Winner and RWAus Ella Award Winner

Hell Squad – SFR Galaxy Award for best Post-Apocalypse for Readers who don't like Post-Apocalypse

The Anomaly Series – #1 Amazon Action Adventure Romance Bestseller

"Like Indiana Jones meets Star Wars. A treasure hunt with a steamy romance." – SFF Dragon, review of *Among Galactic Ruins*

"Strap in, enjoy the heat of romance and the daring of this group of space travellers!" – Di, Top 500 Amazon Reviewer, review of *At Star's End*

"Action, danger, aliens, romance – yup, it's another great book from Anna Hackett!" – Book Gannet Reviews, review of *Hell Squad: Marcus*

Sign up for my VIP mailing list and get your *free box set* containing three action-packed romances.

Visit here to get started:
www.annahackettbooks.com

CHAPTER ONE

She shifted on the chair, causing the chains binding her hands to clank together. Eve Traynor snorted. The wrist and ankle restraints were overkill. She was on a low-orbit prison circling Earth. Where the fuck did they think she was going to go?

Eve shifted her shoulders to try to ease the tension from having her hands tied behind her back. For the millionth time, she studied her surroundings. The medium-sized room was empty, except for her chair. Everything from the floor to the ceiling was dull-gray metal. All of the Citadel Prison was drab and sparse. She'd learned every boring inch of it the last few months.

One wide window provided the only break in the otherwise uniform space. Outside, she caught a tantalizing glimpse of the blue-green orb of Earth below.

Her gut clenched and she drank in the sight of her home. Five months she'd been locked away in this prison. Five months since her life had imploded.

She automatically thought of her sisters. She sucked in a deep breath. She hated everything they'd had to go through because of what had happened. Hell, she thought of her mom as well, even though their last contact had been the day after Eve had been imprisoned. Her mom had left Eve a drunken, scathing message.

The door to the room opened, and Eve lifted her chin and braced.

When she saw the dark-blue Space Corps uniform, she stiffened. When she saw the row of stars on the lapel, she gritted her teeth.

Admiral Linda Barber stepped into the room, accompanied by a female prison guard. The admiral's hair was its usual sleek bob of highlighted, ash-blonde hair. Her brown eyes were steady.

Eve looked at the guard. "Take me back to my cell."

The admiral lifted a hand. "Please leave us."

The guard hesitated. "That's against protocol, ma'am—"

"It'll be fine." The admiral's stern voice said she was giving an order, not making a request.

The guard hesitated again, then ducked through the door. It clicked closed behind her.

Eve sniffed. "Say what you have to say and leave."

Admiral Barber sighed, taking a few steps closer. "I know you're angry. You have a right to be—"

"You think?" Eve sucked back the rush of molten anger. "I got tossed under the fucking starship to save a mama's boy. A mama's boy who had no right to be in command of one of Space Corps' vessels."

Shit. Eve wanted to pummel something. Preferably the face of Robert J. Hathaway—golden son of Rear-Admiral Elisabeth Hathaway. A man who, because of family connections, was given captaincy of the *Orion*, even though he lacked the intelligence and experience needed to lead it.

Meanwhile, Eve—a Space Corps veteran—had worked her ass off during her career in the Corps, and had been promised her own ship, only to be denied her chance. Instead, she'd been assigned as Hathaway's second-in-command. To be a glorified babysitter, and to actually run the ship, just without the title and the pay raise.

She'd swallowed it. Swallowed Hathaway's incompetence and blowhard bullshit. Until he'd fucked up. Big-time.

"The Haumea Incident was regrettable," Barber said.

Eve snorted. "Mostly for the people who died. And

definitely for me, since I'm the one shackled to a chair in the Citadel. Meanwhile, I assume Bobby Hathaway is still a dedicated Space Corps employee."

"He's no longer a captain of a ship. And he never will be again."

"Right. Mommy got him a cushy desk job back at Space Corps Headquarters."

The silence was deafening and it made Eve want to kick something.

"I'm sorry, Eve. We all know what happened wasn't right."

Eve jerked on her chains and they clanked against the chair. "And you let it happen. All of Space Corps leadership did, to appease Mommy Hathaway. I dedicated my life to the Corps, and you all screwed me over for an admiral's incompetent son. I got sentenced to prison for *his* mistakes." Stomach turning in vicious circles, Eve looked at the floor, sucking in air. She stared at the soft booties on her feet. Damned inmate footwear. She wasn't even allowed proper fucking shoes.

Admiral Barber moved to her side. "I'm here to offer you a chance at freedom."

Gaze narrowing, Eve looked up. Barber looked... nervous. Eve had never seen the self-assured woman nervous before.

"There's a mission. If you complete it, you'll be released from prison."

Interesting. "And reinstated? With a full pardon?"

Barber's lips pursed and her face looked pinched. "We can negotiate."

So, no. "Screw your offer." Eve would prefer to rot in her cell, rather than help the Space Corps.

The admiral moved in front of her, her low-heeled pumps echoing on the floor. "Eve, the fate of the world depends on this mission."

Barber's serious tone sent a shiver skating down Eve's spine. She met the woman's brown eyes.

"The Kantos are gathering their forces just beyond the boundary at Station Omega V."

Fuck. The Kantos. The insectoid alien race had been nipping at Earth for years. Their humanoid-insectoid soldiers were the brains of the operation, but they encompassed all manner of ugly, insect-like beasts as well.

With the invention of zero-point drives several decades ago, Earth's abilities for space exploration had exploded. Then, thirty years ago, they'd made first contact with an alien species—the Eon.

The Eon shared a common ancestor with the humans of Earth. They were bigger and broader, with a few differing organs, but generally human-looking. They had larger lungs, a stronger, bigger heart, and a more efficiently-designed digestion system. This gave them increased strength and stamina, which in turn made them excellent warriors. Unfortunately, they also wanted nothing to do with Earth and its inferior Terrans.

The Eon, and their fearsome warriors and warships, stayed inside their own space and had banned Terrans from crossing their boundaries.

Then, twenty years ago, the first unfortunate and bloody meeting with the Kantos had occurred.

Since then, the Kantos had returned repeatedly to

nip at the Terran borders—attacking ships, space stations, and colonies.

But it had become obvious in the last year or so that the Kantos had something bigger planned. The Haumea Incident had made that crystal clear.

The Kantos wanted Earth. There were to be no treaties, alliances, or negotiations. They wanted to descend like locusts and decimate everything—all the planet's resources, and most of all, the humans.

Yes, the Kantos wanted to freaking use humans as a food source. Eve suppressed a shudder.

"And?" she said.

"We have to do whatever it takes to save our planet."

Eve tilted her head. "The Eon."

Admiral Barber smiled. "You were always sharp, Eve. Yes, the Eon are the only ones with the numbers, the technology, and the capability to help us repel the Kantos."

"Except they want nothing to do with us." No one had seen or spoken with an Eon for three decades.

"Desperate times call for desperate measures."

Okay, Eve felt that shiver again. She felt like she was standing on the edge of a platform, about to be shoved under the starship again.

"What's the mission?" she asked carefully.

"We want you to abduct War Commander Davion Thann-Eon."

Holy fuck. Eve's chest clenched so tight she couldn't even draw a breath. Then the air rushed into her lungs, and she threw her head back and laughed. Tears ran down her face.

"You're kidding."

But the admiral wasn't laughing.

Eve shook her head. "That's a fucking suicide mission. You want me to abduct the deadliest, most decorated Eon war commander who controls the largest, most destructive Eon warship in their fleet?"

"Yes."

"No."

"Eve, you have a record of making...risky decisions."

Eve shook her head. "I always calculate the risks."

"Yes, but you use a higher margin of error than the rest of us."

"I've always completed my missions successfully." The Haumea Incident excluded, since that was Bobby's brilliant screw-up.

"Yes. That's why we know if anyone has a chance of making this mission a success, it's you."

"I may as well take out a blaster and shoot myself right now. One, I'll never make it into Eon space, let alone aboard the *Desteron*."

Since the initial encounter, they'd collected whatever intel they could on the Eon. Eve had seen secret schematics of that warship. And she had to admit, the thought of being aboard that ship left her a little damp between her thighs. She loved space and flying, and the big, sleek warship was something straight out of her fantasies.

"We have an experimental, top-of-the-line stealth ship for you to use," the admiral said.

Eve carried on like the woman hadn't spoken. "And two, even if I got close to the war commander, he's bigger and stronger than me, not to mention bonded to a fucking deadly alien symbiont that gives him added strength and the ability to create organic armor and weapons with a single thought. I'd be dead in seconds."

"We recovered a…substance that is able to contain the symbiont the Eon use."

Eve narrowed her eyes. "Recovered from where?"

Admiral Barber cleared her throat. "From the wreck of a Kantos ship. It was clearly tech they were developing to use against the Eon."

Shit. "So I'm to abduct the war commander, and then further enrage him by neutralizing his symbiont."

"We believe the containment is temporary, and there is an antidote."

Eve shook her head. "This is beyond insane."

"For the fate of humanity, we have to try."

"*Talk* to them," Eve said. "Use some diplomacy."

"We tried. They refused all contact."

Because humans were simply ants to the Eon. Small, insignificant, an annoyance.

Although, truth be told, humanity only had itself to blame. By all accounts, Terrans hadn't behaved very well at first contact. The meetings with the Eon had turned into blustering threats, different countries trying to make alliances with the aliens while happily stabbing each other in the back.

Now Earth wanted to abduct an Eon war commander. No, not a war commander, *the* war commander. So dumb. She wished she had a hand free so she could slap it over her eyes.

"Find another sacrificial lamb."

The admiral was silent for a long moment. "If you won't do it for yourself or for humanity, then do it for your sisters."

Eve's blood chilled and she cocked her head. "What's this got to do with my sisters?"

"They've made a lot of noise about your imprisonment. Agitating for your freedom."

Eve breathed through her nose. God, she loved her sisters. Still, she didn't know whether to be pleased or pissed. "And?"

"Your sister has shared some classified information with the press about the Haumea Incident."

Eve fought back a laugh. Lara wasn't shy about sharing her thoughts about this entire screwed-up situation. Eve's older sister was a badass Space Corps special forces marine. Lara wouldn't hesitate to take down anyone who pissed her off, the Space Corps included.

"And she had access to information she should not have had access to, meaning your other sister has done some...creative hacking."

Dammit. The rush of love was mixed with some annoyance. Sweet, geeky Wren had a giant, super-smart brain. She was a computer-systems engineer for some company with cutting-edge technology in Japan. It helped keep her baby sister's big brain busy, because Wren hadn't found a computer she couldn't hack.

"Plenty of people are unhappy with what your sisters have been stirring up," Barber continued.

Eve stiffened. She didn't like where this was going.

"I've tried to run interference—"

"Admiral—"

Barber held up a hand. "I can't keep protecting them, Eve. I've been trying, but some of this is even above my pay grade. If you don't do this mission, powers outside of my control will go after them. They'll both end up in a cell right alongside yours until the Kantos arrive and blow this prison out of the sky."

Her jaw tight, Eve's brain turned all the information over. *Fucking fuck.*

"Eve, if there is anyone who has a chance of succeeding on this mission, it's you."

Eve stayed silent.

Barber stepped closer. "I don't care if you do it for yourself, the billions of people of Earth, or your sisters—"

"I'll do it." The words shot out of Eve, harsh and angry.

She'd do it—abduct the scariest alien war commander in the galaxy—for all the reasons the admiral listed—to clear her name, for her freedom, to save the world, and for the sisters she loved.

Honestly, it didn't matter anyway, because the odds of her succeeding and coming back alive were zero.

EVE LEFT THE STARSHIP GYM, towel around her neck, and her muscles warm and limber from her workout.

God, it was nice to work out when it suited her. On the Citadel Prison, exercise time was strictly scheduled, monitored, and timed.

Two crew members came into view, heading down

the hall toward her. As soon as the uniformed men spotted her, they looked at the floor and passed her quickly.

Eve rolled her eyes. Well, she wasn't aboard the *Polaris* to make friends, and she had to admit, she had a pretty notorious reputation. She'd never been one to blindly follow the rules, plus there was the Haumea Incident and her imprisonment. And her family were infamous in the Space Corps. Her father had been a space marine, killed in action in one of the early Kantos encounters. Her mom had been a decorated Space Corps member, but after Eve's dad had died, her mom had started drinking. It had deteriorated until she'd gone off the rails. She'd done it quite publicly, blaming the Space Corps for her husband's death. In the process, she'd forgotten she had three young, grieving girls.

Yep, Eve was well aware that the people you cared for most either left you, or let you down. The employer you worked your ass off for treated you like shit. The only two people in the galaxy that didn't apply to were her sisters.

Eve pushed thoughts of her parents away. Instead, she scanned the starship. The *Polaris* was a good ship. A mid-size cruiser, she was designed for exploration, but well-armed as well. Eve guessed they'd be heading out beyond Neptune about now.

The plan was for the *Polaris* to take her to the edge of Eon space, where she'd take a tiny, two-person stealth ship, sneak up to the *Desteron*, then steal onboard.

Piece of cake. She rolled her eyes.

Back in her small cabin, she took a quick shower,

dressed, and then headed to the ops room. It was a small room close to the bridge that the ship's captain had made available to her.

She stepped inside, and all the screens flickered to life. A light table stood in the center of the room, and everything was filled with every scrap of intel that the Space Corps had on the Eon Empire, their warriors, the *Desteron*, and War Commander Thann-Eon.

It was more than she'd guessed. A lot of it had been classified. There was fascinating intel on the four Eon homeworld planets—Eon, Jad, Felis, and Ath. Each Eon warrior carried their homeworld in their name, along with their clan names. The war commander hailed from the planet Eon, and Thann was a clan known as a warrior clan.

Eve swiped her fingers across the light table and studied pictures of the *Desteron*. They were a few years old and taken from a great distance, but that didn't hide the warship's power.

It was fearsome. Black, sleek, and impressive. It was built for speed and stealth, but also power. It had to be packed with weapons beyond their imagination.

She touched the screen again and slid the image to the side. Another image appeared—the only known picture of War Commander Thann-Eon.

Jesus. The man packed a punch. All Eon warriors looked alike—big, broad-shouldered, muscular. They all had longish hair—not quite reaching the shoulders, but not cut short, either. Their hair usually ranged from dark brown to a tawny, golden-brown. There was no black or blond hair among the Eon. Their skin color ranged from dark-brown to light-brown, as well.

Before first contact had gone sour, both sides had done some DNA testing, and confirmed the Eon and Terrans shared an ancestor.

The war commander was wearing a pitch-black, sleeveless uniform. He was tall, built, with long legs and powerful thighs. He was exactly the kind of man you expected to stride onto a battlefield, pull a sword, and slaughter everyone. He had a strong face, one that shouted power. Eve stroked a finger over the image. He had a square jaw, a straight, almost aggressive nose, and a well-formed brow. His eyes were as dark as space, but shot through with intriguing threads of blue.

"It's you and me, War Commander." If he didn't kill her, first.

Suddenly, sirens blared.

Eve didn't stop to think. She slammed out of the ops room and sprinted onto the bridge.

Inside, the large room was a flurry of activity.

Captain Chen stood in the center of the space, barking orders at his crew.

Her heart contracted. God, she'd missed this so much. The vibration of the ship beneath her feet, her team around her, even the scent of recycled starship air.

"You shouldn't be in here," a sharp voice snapped.

Eve turned, locking gazes with the stocky, bearded XO. Sub-Captain Porter wasn't a fan of hers.

"Leave her," Captain Chen told his second-in-command. "She's seen more Kantos ships than all of us combined."

The captain looked back at his team. "Shields up."

Eve studied the screen and the Kantos ship approaching.

It looked like a bug. It had large, outstretched legs, and a bulky, segmented, central fuselage. It wasn't the biggest ship she'd seen, but it wasn't small, either. It was probably out on some intel mission.

"Sir," a female voice called out. "We're getting a distress call from the *Panama*, a cargo ship en route to Nightingale Space Station. They're under attack from a swarm of small Kantos ships."

Eve sucked in a breath, her hand curling into a fist. This was a usual Kantos tactic. They would overwhelm a ship with their small swarm ships. It had ugly memories of the Haumea Incident stabbing at her.

"Open the comms channel," the captain ordered.

"Please...help us." A harried man's voice came over the distorted comm line. "...can't hold out much...thirty-seven crew onboard...we are..."

Suddenly, a huge explosion of light flared in the distance.

Eve's shoulders sagged. The cargo ship was gone.

"Goddammit," the XO bit out.

The front legs of the larger Kantos ship in front of them started to glow orange.

"They're going to fire," Eve said.

The captain straightened. "Evasive maneuvers."

His crew raced to obey the orders, the *Polaris* veering suddenly to the right.

"The swarm ships will be on their way back." Eve knew the Kantos loved to swarm like locusts.

"Release the tridents," the captain said.

Good. Eve watched the small, triple-pronged space mines rain out the side of the ship. They'd be a dangerous minefield for the Kantos swarm.

The main Kantos ship swung around.

"They're locking weapons," someone shouted.

Eve fought the need to shout out orders and offer the captain advice. Last time she'd done that, she'd ended up in shackles.

The blast hit the *Polaris*, the shields lighting up from the impact. The ship shuddered.

"Shields holding, but depleting," another crew member called out.

"Sub-Captain Traynor?" The captain's dark gaze met hers.

Something loosened in her chest. "It's a raider-class cruiser, Captain. You're smaller and more maneuverable. You need to circle around it, spray it with laser fire. Its weak spots are on the sides. Sustained laser fire will eventually tear it open. You also need to avoid the legs."

"Fly circles around it?" a young man at a console said. "That's crazy."

Eve eyed the lead pilot. "You up for this?"

The man swallowed. "I don't think I can..."

"Sure you can, if you want us to survive this."

"Walker, do it," the captain barked.

The pilot pulled in a breath and the *Polaris* surged forward. They rounded the Kantos ship. Up close, the bronze-brown hull looked just like the carapace of an insect. One of the legs swung up, but Walker had quick reflexes.

"Fire," Eve said.

The weapons officer started firing. Laser fire hit the Kantos ship in a pretty row of orange.

"Keep going," Eve urged.

They circled the ship, firing non-stop.

Eve crossed her arms over her chest. Everything in her was still, but alive, filled with energy. She'd always known she was born to stand on the bridge of a starship.

"More," she urged. "Keep firing."

"Swarm ships incoming," a crew member yelled.

"Hold," Eve said calmly. "Trust the mines." She eyed the perspiring weapons officer. "What's your name, Lieutenant?"

"Law, ma'am. Lieutenant Miriam Law."

"You're doing fine, Law. Ignore the swarm ships and keep firing on the cruiser."

The swarm ships rushed closer, then hit the field of mines. Eve saw the explosions, like brightly colored pops of fireworks.

The lasers kept cutting into the hull of the larger Kantos ship. She watched the ship's engines fire. They were going to try and make a run for it.

"Bring us around, Walker. Fire everything you have, Law."

They swung around to face the side of the Kantos ship straight on. The laser ripped into the hull.

There was a blinding flash of light, and startled exclamations filled the bridge. She squinted until the light faded away.

On the screen, the Kantos ship broke up into pieces.

Captain Chen released a breath. "Thank you, Sub-Captain."

Eve inclined her head. She glanced at the silent crew. "Good flying, Walker. And excellent shooting, Law."

But she looked back at the screen, at the debris hanging in space and the last of the swarm ships retreating.

They'd keep coming. No matter what. It was ingrained in the Kantos to destroy.

They had to be stopped.

CHAPTER TWO

War Commander Davion Thann-Eon strode down the corridor of his warship, boots echoing on the black metal floor.

He passed several warriors, and as soon as they saw him, they snapped to attention.

He nodded at them and kept moving. When he stepped onto his bridge, he scanned the tiered levels and stations manned by his elite warriors.

"War Commander on the bridge," his second-in-command called out.

Gazes swung his way, spines snapped straight.

Davion lifted a hand and waved at them. They all turned back to their screens.

Every warrior wore the same outfit that Davion did—black pants tucked into boots, with a sleeveless, fitted black shirt that stretched over muscled bodies. Davion had several blue, circular pips on his collar denoting his rank, and the others had less or different designs depending on their rank and functions.

He was the youngest war commander in Eon history. From the day he'd entered the Eon Military Academy, he'd excelled and outstripped his fellow recruits. He was exceptionally good at what he did, and dedicated to protecting the Eon Empire.

"Ready for your vacation?"

The deep voice made him look at Brack, his second and one of his closest friends. It was almost like looking in a mirror.

Brack Thann-Felis was the same height as Davion, slightly leaner, with the exact same shade of dark-brown hair and the same blue-black eyes. He was from the Thann clan, so that explained the similar looks, but his family hailed from the planet Felis.

"I'm looking forward to hunting." Davion couldn't remember the last time he'd had any days off. His job was a busy one and when he wasn't aboard the *Desteron* or engaged in military operations, there were always meetings, treaties to sign, strategic operations to plan. His life was his work, what he was good at, and his people had his loyalty.

Brack rolled his eyes. "Most warriors head to a pleasure planet for vacation, Davion. They swim, eat, and fuck. They do not head to the most dangerous hunter planet in the quadrant."

Davion smiled. "You know I like a challenge." No, he *loved* a challenge. He loved pushing himself to the limit, physically and mentally.

Brack shook his head, his long hair brushing his jaw.

"Anything to report?" Davion asked.

Brack's face turned serious. "Yes. Caze?"

Caze Vann-Jad stepped forward. His hair was longer, framing a sharply handsome face, and his eyes were threaded with silver. Caze was the warrior any Eon would want at their back in a fight. All Eon were muscular, but the Security Commander's body was honed to a weapon.

"Long-range scanners picked up a Kantos signature," Caze said.

Davion scowled. He detested the hungry, greedy, disorganized Kantos. They used their numbers to overwhelm, and possessed little strategy or skill.

"In Eon space?"

Caze shook his head. "Just beyond. Looks like they had a skirmish with a Terran ship."

Davion grunted. "Outcome?"

"The swarm ships destroyed one Terran ship. A second Terran ship destroyed both the majority of the swarm ships and a raider-class cruiser."

Hmm, the Terrans were proving far more tenacious than the Eon leadership had first thought.

Davion had been a boy when the Eon had first encountered the closely related species. He heard all the stories of the Terrans' lack of discipline, hedonism, stubbornness, and infighting. The old Eon king had blocked all relations with them, and banned them from entering Eon space.

Davion wasn't fond of leaving any species to be decimated by the Kantos, but he had his orders. Despite clear signs that the Kantos were gearing up for a large assault,

Earth was on its own. The Eon had their own empire to defend, and the Kantos weren't the only aggressive species with war on their minds.

"Monitor the situation and keep me informed," Davion said. "Engineering?"

"All functioning normally," Brack said.

"Weapons."

"Normal," Caze answered. "And the upgrade to the pulse cannon array is going well."

"Excellent." Davion looked at Brack. "You'll take care of my ship while I'm away."

Brack's lips lifted. "I find your chair very comfortable."

Davion bared his teeth. "Don't get too comfortable, old friend."

"And don't get yourself killed on Hunter7."

Davion felt a lick of anticipation. Hunter7 was one of the synthetic warrior-training planets—the hardest level designed to offer a warrior the ultimate challenge. It was where the top recruits were sent to test their skills, and where experienced warriors went to keep their skills sharp. Davion went there for fun.

"I'll be in my office to finish some work, then the gym. Once we're in range of Hunter7, I'll fly myself down."

Brack nodded. "I'll ensure that your private shuttle is prepared and fueled. We'll see you in a week." His second shook his head. "I still think you're crazy to pit yourself against killer wildlife, rather than get a tan and bury yourself between some curvy thighs."

Davion grunted.

On patrol, warriors were dedicated to the job. But on

their time off...they often found company of the temporary variety. They rarely married or mated. He had non-warrior friends back on Eon who had married, and very few who'd been lucky enough to meet their mate—their perfect biological match. For decades, mating had happened less and less for the Eon, and warriors were only fertile with their mates. To ensure the survival of the Eon species, their top scientists used the DNA of the best and brightest to ensure married couples had children.

Davion had been asked to donate his own DNA several times, but something had held him back. He still held the old-fashioned notion of wanting to raise his own children.

But romantic relationships and marriage weren't very compatible with military life. For warriors, the pinnacle of their military careers involved years aboard warships, bloody confrontations with hostile species, and fierce training. Davion had no time for females and children. Besides, he'd never met a female who could tempt him away from the job he was born to do.

Occasionally, he visited pleasure planets. More often, he sweated off any sexual frustration with hunting, training, or his hand.

"Let me worry about where I bury my body parts, Brack."

Brack snapped his boots together. "Yes, War Commander."

Davion stopped himself from popping his fist into his second's gut. He shook his head. "See you in a week."

EVE SAT at the controls of the small stealth ship, enjoying finally being alone and in control of her own craft.

What she wasn't going to enjoy was breaking into the ship dominating her viewscreen.

There it was. The *Desteron*. The most powerful warship known to humans.

Ever since she'd crossed into Eon space, her nerves were stretched so tight she felt like she was going to snap. The closer she got to the ship, the more tense she felt. God, the warship was something.

It had a black hull that looked like it absorbed all light, like a black hole. The front was rounded, but the back tapered in to where the engines sat. It made her think of some smooth ocean predator. The Eon sure knew how to build a warship.

She swallowed. Any second now, the *Desteron* could pick up her ship's signature. Admiral Barber was sure the stealth capabilities of the ship would keep her cloaked, but no one had tested the *Desteron's* systems before. And Terran tech was nothing compared to Eon tech.

She was well aware that she was unlikely to survive this encounter. War Commander Thann-Eon was a decorated warrior. He was not only an exceptional leader, but a battle-strategy expert, and also known for being a hell of a fighter.

Eve blew out a breath. Added to that, all Eon warriors were bonded to an alien symbiont known as a helian. Space Corps knew very little about the symbionts, but they did know it gave the warriors abilities that made them near-unstoppable in battle. That included organic armor, and weapons the warrior could activate and change at will. She'd only read about the helian but she thought it sounded awesome.

She watched as the *Desteron* got bigger and bigger on-screen. *Don't spot me. Don't spot me. Just a friendly little stealth ship doing stealthy things.* Her throat was tight, and any second now, she expected her ship to be blown out of space.

Her heart pounded against her ribs. *Thud. Thud. Thud.*

Soon, all Eve could see in the viewscreen was the black hull. She'd studied every scrap of intel on the ship, and she'd had to extrapolate and make a few assumptions. She was planning to attach her ship close to an underside exhaust port on the *Desteron* and hoped that blocked any signature her ship might give off. Then she was going to cut her way in.

If she managed to make it aboard, then she'd have to navigate the ship and its crew.

She blew out a breath. She knew next to nothing about the interior of the warship, so she was going to have to wing it. Luckily, winging it was what Eve did best.

Clang.

She palmed the screen and felt the stealth ship's MagnaLocks attach. She rose from her chair.

She'd made it. Now the fun began.

Eve wore the latest in Space Corps space suits. It was slick, mostly black with touches of white, and designed for special forces marines. It could repel a fair bit of damage, wouldn't hamper her movements in a fight, and monitored her vitals.

She grabbed her favorite StrikeFire laser blaster and holstered it. Then she grabbed her RaptorClaw knife and slid it into her belt. She patted them. She loved her babies.

Next, Eve added a few PlastiCuff restraints and hoped to hell they were strong enough to hold an enraged Eon warrior. She also checked the small kit that Admiral Barber had given her.

The small metallic case held three injectors. One was filled with a black, sticky ooze. Her nose wrinkled. Using anything Kantos-related grated on her. But the admiral had assured her that the ooze would contain a helian, which meant an Eon warrior couldn't use his armor or weapons.

The second injector held a bright orange fluid. This was the antidote to the ooze. Just one drop would dissolve the ooze away. The third was a clear sedative that Barber told her *should* knock out an Eon warrior.

"Should" didn't fill Eve with much confidence. She tucked the kit into her belt.

Then she moved to the hatch and opened it. She stared at the black hull of the *Desteron* and touched it with her gloved hand. It had a faint, scale-like pattern.

Her gut cramped. Just like it was rumored the Eon warriors' armor had. God, please don't let the hull be part alien symbiont. If it was, they'd already know she was there.

But so far, it appeared she was undetected. She pulled out her BurnCutter, the small device sitting in the palm of her hand. She pressed it to the metal and then watched it attach. Lights flashed as the device activated, then it started burning through the hull and moving in a circle.

This is for you, Lara and Wren. Be safe.

It had always been the Traynor sisters against the world. After their father had died and their mother had imploded and gotten booted out of the Space Corps, they'd lost their father's pension. Things had been tough after that. When she was sober enough, Mika Traynor had been out working—mainly in private security or as a club bouncer. That had left the sisters alone a lot. It had fallen on the girls to keep their home together.

They'd been known as badass Lara, tough Eve, and sweet, smart Wren.

The BurnCutter made a low beep. Eve waited a second, knowing the device was creating a seal between the two ships. A longer beep and she knew it was finished. She grabbed the device and slid it onto her belt. She watched as the metal circle disintegrated in a puff of ash, leaving a perfect hole. She ducked through it and onto the *Desteron*.

She looked around and smiled. Score one for Eve. She might not know the interior of the *Desteron*, but she knew ships. Just as she'd suspected, she'd boarded right near the engine room. She found herself in one corner of the large space.

She pressed another device, a HoloCamo, to the hull behind her, and a holographic shimmer flowed over the hole. It camouflaged the breach to look like the rest of the wall. *Perfect.*

Eve turned, ducking down, and stealthily moved through the engine room. It was fascinating. She stared briefly at the sleek bits of moving equipment, strange gauges, and small vats of bright-blue fluid. Machinery chugged, and Eve wove her way under several organic-looking pipes and black metal parts. Other pieces of equipment were smooth, black metal and soundless, giving her no clue as to what their function was.

God, she could stay here all day, investigating everything. She'd be a very happy woman.

But she turned her head away from the alien technology, her gaze narrowing. She had a mission to complete.

She moved quickly until she reached the back wall of the engine room. Her plan was to use the maintenance-access conduits to move through the ship. All ships needed space for crew to access hard-to-reach systems and equipment.

Eve eased along the wall, searching for some sort of entrance. *Come on.*

There. She spotted the small door at eye level. Probably an easy climb in for a six-foot-plus Eon warrior. She moved closer, readying to open it, when she heard voices. Deep voices. Getting closer.

Shit. She ducked behind some equipment, and pressed as close to it as she could. Waves of heat radiated off it but it wasn't hot enough to burn. She kept very still, listening as the voices grew in volume. Then, for the first time in her life, Eve saw an Eon warrior in the flesh.

Her chest locked. *Holy space dust.*

The photos she'd seen did them no justice. They were big, muscled, and freaking gorgeous.

Eve was the first to admit she liked a built guy. She couldn't care less about a pretty face, though. Instead, she liked knowing a man could handle himself and at least put up a bit of a fight if she challenged him.

Through a crack between two vats, she watched the warriors as they studied some piece of equipment. She definitely wouldn't call these guys pretty by any means, with their rugged, strong features, but they absolutely held a lot of appeal.

She also got a good look at the broad shoulders and long legs covered by their standard black uniforms. They had no sleeves and their shirts were practically suctioned on to their hard chests. Both had longish hair—one in a deep brown, and the other tawnier.

The warriors studied the equipment, turning dials and flipping switches, talking to each other in a low murmur.

Eve had a neural translator implanted behind her left ear—like all Space Corps members—but the warriors weren't close enough for her to make out what they were saying.

Finally, after what felt like an eternity, the men moved off.

She released a long breath. Now that she'd had a good look at the warriors, she had grave doubts about taking one of them down.

Especially the war commander.

She was going to need the element of surprise, otherwise the warrior would snap her neck with a flick of his wrist.

She waited a few more minutes until she was sure the warriors had completely moved away. She jumped up and eased back to the maintenance conduit. She leaped up, pressing her boots to the wall on either side of the door. The magnetic soles activated, holding her in place. Eve pulled out her AllDriver tool and set to work on the screws. A moment later, she opened the door.

Shit, it was small. She peered into the tight, horizontal space. No way a warrior would fit in here.

Suddenly, a small whizzing noise made her stiffen. A small maintenance robot zoomed down the corridor. It paused right in front of Eve, then turned, and zoomed away. Well, that explained why the space wasn't very large.

She climbed through the opening, and replaced the door behind her. She clicked on the flashlight attached to the shoulder of her suit.

Okay, it was definitely a tight fit, but she'd make it.

Again, she'd had to make some assumptions on where she'd find the war commander's cabin. What little intel they did have suggested it was close to the bridge. That's right where Eve would want to be, if the *Desteron* was her ship.

She hoped War Commander Thann-Eon felt the same.

Eve started crawling.

CHAPTER THREE

Davion strode into his quarters, stripping off his training gear. He'd had a long, hard workout in the ship's gym. His body felt warm and loose, and he already felt more relaxed.

The ship was now in range of Hunter7 and anticipation slid along his veins.

He crossed his cabin, headed for his washroom. His bags were already packed and on his private shuttle. As soon as he'd washed and changed, he was leaving.

Halfway across his cabin, something skittered across his senses. He felt his helian stir, his senses expanding. He paused and scanned his quarters.

Nothing was out of place in his cabin. He liked things tidy.

He shook his head. Clearly, he was just ready for his vacation. He shucked the last of his clothes and headed for the shower. In the stall, mist rose around him. He was going to enjoy a long swim on Hunter7—much better than the mist of a starship water-conservation shower.

Davion kept his washing quick—a habit bred into him after years of starship living. As he exited the stall, he grabbed a super-absorbent towel, wiping the water off his skin. Then naked, he strode back into his cabin, heading for his closet.

Again, he felt a prickle of unease across the back of his neck, and he frowned.

He shook his head once more. He *really* needed some time off, if he was imagining threats in his own quarters.

The attack came from nowhere.

A firm weight hit his back and Davion stumbled.

By Cren's black heart. He went down on one knee, and an arm slid around his neck and pulled backward.

The pressure cut off his air. Shoving his surprise aside, he reached back and grabbed at his assailant. His hands slid over a shiny suit. Whoever it was, they were small.

But they were also cunning. His attacker moved, pushing their weight back, which put more pressure on the arm across Davion's throat. He coughed, fighting for air.

His attacker reached around with a slim arm and slapped something over his helian. The black, gel-like substance oozed over the wristband that housed his symbiont. *Cren*.

Davion tried to activate his helian, calling for his armor and weapons, but nothing happened. Whatever the black gunk was, it cut him off from his symbiont.

A punch of anger inside him. It didn't matter, he didn't need his armor to take down his attacker. He might be naked, but he wasn't helpless.

Davion surged up, his attacker clinging to his back. He spun and slammed his assailant into the wall. The arm around his neck loosened.

Then Davion reached over his shoulder and grabbed a handful of what felt like his attacker's hair. He heard a sharp gasp. Then he yanked them over his head.

The small figure flew through the air and hit his bed, rolling instantly up on their knees.

Davion got a good look at a pair of brilliant blue eyes. He froze.

A *woman*.

She was slender, but the slick, black-and-white suit left no doubt that she was also fit. Dark hair was pulled back severely from a face with a pointed chin and high cheekbones.

She was Terran.

In a blur, she moved, launching at him. She aimed a fist at his gut and Davion blocked it, only to realize that he'd done exactly what she wanted.

He left his upper body dipped and open. She leaped up and landed a hard hit to the back of his neck. He grunted, and in that split second, she jumped on him. Two toned thighs circled his neck.

Her slim, strong body twisted, and they both crashed to the floor.

Davion growled. *Enough*.

He had questions—like how the Cren she was on his

ship, in his cabin, and why—and she was going to give him the answers.

He shifted, ready to pin her to the floor, when he felt a sharp sting at his neck.

"I'm really sorry," she said in a deep, throaty voice.

Davion felt a tingle flow through his veins. A drug. *By Ston's sword.*

He turned his head, and his gaze met hers.

"Just for the record—" she said "—I was against this plan."

"You'll...pay..." It was difficult to speak, and his vision was blurring.

She winced. "Yeah, I know."

As his muscles went lax, she leaped off him and helped lower him flat on the floor. He glared at her, unable to move any of his limbs.

"You should be out by now," she muttered.

"Make...you regret this."

"I already do." Her gaze drifted down his naked body.

He saw the flare of appreciation in her eyes before she looked away.

She cleared her throat. "If I had a choice..."

He heard the regret in her voice, but his thoughts were all splintering, too hard to pull together. He stared into those amazing blue eyes, like they were a lifeline.

Brack would never let him live this down. Him, the greatest war commander of the Eon fleet, taken down by a woman. A small, Terran one.

Then Davion lost consciousness.

DAMN, he was a heavy bastard.

Eve had managed to pull some trousers onto the war commander. That had been a very hard job, considering he was dead weight. And especially when she was trying not to notice his nakedness.

His impressive nakedness.

With a lot of grunting and groaning, she'd gotten him covered enough. So maybe she'd looked at the smooth skin of his chest and the smattering of brown hair on it, once or twice. And the hard abdomen. She'd managed to drag him into the maintenance conduit that ran alongside his cabin. Thank the stars that it was larger than the ones down near the engine room. Still, it was a very tight fit.

In the narrow tunnel, she leaned over and sucked in some air. No way she could get him all the way back to her ship. He was too damn big and heavy.

Plus, she had no idea how long the sedative she'd used on him would last. It had taken far longer than she'd expected for it to knock him out.

She pulled out the PlastiCuffs she'd brought and tied his hands together. His wrists were thick and strong. One was covered in the device she'd used to trap his symbiont. The sticky substance had the faint scent of tar and smoke. Her gaze fell on his hands—they were big too, with long fingers and blunt nails.

Focus on the job, Eve. She snapped the cuffs on. They were the highest rated, and she hoped to hell they would hold an enraged alien warrior.

Right. Now, she needed a Plan B. Fast.

She heard a chime, and realized there was some sort of communicator attached to his trousers.

"War Commander, I know you're preparing to depart for your vacation." The voice was deep and smooth. "I just wanted to leave you a message to let you know that your private shuttle is prepped and fueled in docking bay AC-7. Good travels, and good hunting."

The communicator clicked off.

Private shuttle. AC-7. She scanned the narrow conduit. She'd passed a few maintenance comp panels earlier. Turning sideways, she shimmied along until she spotted a panel. She pried it open and saw a comp screen embedded in the wall. A few swipes activated it, and it took her a while to wade through the data. She'd learned the Eon lexicon at the Space Corps Academy. *There.* A map. She scrolled through and a shiver of excitement went through her. An entire, detailed map of the *Desteron*. Ooh, she was so downloading a copy of this.

She tapped on the screen and quickly found Bay AC-7. Her pulse leaped. It was right next door.

Heading back to the war commander's prone form, she pulled another device off her belt. She touched a button on the LoadLifter, and a small, strong cable wound out. It was a small cargo-carrying device. She wrapped the cable around the warrior. When she pressed another button, the lifter did most of the heavy-lifting and, as she moved, it took most of the warrior's weight.

She still had to pull, but it was far easier now. She dragged him down the conduit and soon they reached the doorway into the docking bay.

Eve quickly grabbed her AllDriver, it whizzed on the

screws, and then she pushed the door open. She peered inside. It was a small bay, neat and orderly. Everything was quiet.

She touched another device on her belt, jamming any cameras in range.

Then she quickly pushed the war commander out of the doorway. "Sorry."

She watched him drop the meter and a half to the ground and winced. Then she climbed down behind him. Grabbing the LoadLifter, she dragged him toward the sexy, little shuttle parked nearby.

Even with the LoadLifter, her arms were starting to burn. "God, why do you have to be so big and muscular?"

When he woke up, he was going to be pissed. As she pulled him around some cargo crates, she blew out a breath. She couldn't worry about that right now. Across the cargo bay, she eyed the shuttle again, and stifled a little moan. It was made of black metal, had a long, sinuous shape, and two arches of metal at the back that formed part of the propulsion system. Yep, the Eon knew how to design sexy ships.

And men.

Eve shut that thought down. That was what five months in prison got you—horny.

Note to self—don't drool over the alien war commander who's going to try and wring your neck when he wakes up.

She pulled him up the ramp of the shuttle and used his palm to open the door. It hissed open, and she tugged him on board.

Oh yeah, baby. The inside was as sleek and sexy as

the outside. She dragged the war commander over to a chair and, with a lot of heaving and grunting, got him into it and strapped in.

Then Eve moved to the cockpit and sat behind the controls. The large pilot's seat enveloped her.

She was a pretty good pilot, but much of this ship was foreign. She'd also heard that Eon warriors used their symbiont to plug into a ship's systems and help them fly.

Well, she didn't have a symbiont, but she was sure as hell going to fly this thing. She shifted around in the large chair, disliking that its size made her feel like a kid playing dress-up. She touched the controls.

Lights flared.

"Automatic takeoff sequence initialized," the computer's voice intoned.

Uh, okay. That was probably a good thing.

"Heading to preset destination, Hunter7."

Hmm. Eve had no idea what Hunter7 was. Still, she'd worry about getting off the *Desteron*, first, then she'd worry about changing course after.

"Automatic takeoff sequence commencing."

The shuttle's engines fired up, a faint vibration going through the ship. More lights flared on the console.

All right, baby. It looked like they were taking off.

Once she put some distance between them and the warship, then she'd work out how to actually fly this thing and make the rendezvous with the *Polaris*. She glanced back at the warrior. He was still passed out in the chair.

Ahead, the cargo bay doors opened, and the shuttle rose from the floor. They zoomed out, going fast.

Eve laughed. She *liked* this shuttle.

They flew out into the dark of space, leaving the *Desteron* behind them.

"Commencing journey to Hunter7," the computer intoned.

Good. Eve still felt twitchy knowing they were in range of the *Desteron*. Each second eased some of the tension inside her. She wondered what this Hunter7 was.

Eve tapped the screen, calling up the information. A picture of a small planet appeared. It had weird signatures, and she leaned forward to study its scans, her brow scrunched. She'd never seen scans like this before.

She glanced at the war commander again. He was still out. She took a second to study his rugged face. He looked younger than she'd expected. Oh, there were a few intriguing lines on his face that said he was used to command and responsibility, but she'd expected someone with his reputation to be far older.

She glanced out of the shuttle's viewscreen. A small, rocky moon had appeared in the distance. They circled around it, and she spotted a green planet straight ahead.

Hunter7.

Okay, soon she was going to need to take over control of the shuttle and change their course. The *Polaris* was waiting for her to bring back the abducted war commander.

But she had to be sure the *Desteron* wouldn't detect her course change. For now, she was going to bask in the fact that she'd succeeded on her mission and was still alive.

She smiled again, then felt a wave of something in the

air. The hairs on the back of her neck rose. She glanced at the war commander and her stomach dropped away.

She found herself staring into a pair of molten, blue-black eyes.

CHAPTER FOUR

Davion woke, instantly aware of his surroundings. He was in his shuttle. His body was sluggish and his hands were tied with restraints. There was also the sweet scent of female in the air.

He glared at his abductor. She was piloting the shuttle. *His* shuttle.

As though she heard his thoughts, she looked his way, smiling, but when her gaze collided with his, her smile dissolved.

Yes, you should be afraid, little thief. "You've made a terrible mistake."

"Oh, I know. But it wasn't my choice." She waved a hand through the air. "Man, I can practically feel the anger radiating off you."

It was his helian. The symbiont amplified emotion, and warriors were taught from a young age how to control it. But right now, control was beyond Davion.

Her tone was unrepentant. A part of him admired her courage, but he was also furious with her.

"This is an outrage," Davion said. "You sneak onto my warship—"

The woman held up a finger. "Unnoticed, I might add."

His anger surged. "And attacked me. You abducted an Eon war commander—"

The finger came up again. "And got away with it."

Davion sucked in a breath. He was used to respect, awe, even fear. He was *not* used to a female who looked at him with none of those things.

Especially considering she was a Terran female.

"Why?" he growled.

She looked up from the controls and raised her eyebrows. "Not for shits and giggles, that's for sure."

He frowned at the strange words. "What?"

She waved a hand at him. "Just an Earth saying. My people want to talk to you."

"This is *not* the way to go about it."

She snorted. "You don't say. Your people wouldn't answer any of Earth's attempts at communication."

"The Eon have no interest in Earth."

"Yes, yes, I know, we're small and technologically inferior. Well, because of your stubborn, elitist refusal to talk, here I am, blackmailed into this debacle."

Davion eyed her. "Blackmailed?"

Something skidded over her face and she looked away.

"This is why my people have no interest in Earth," he

said. "You fight amongst yourselves, you're chaotic, you have no focus—"

"Oh, so you're so perfect?" The woman's bright-blue gaze ran over his bare chest. She didn't look impressed.

Davion straightened. "You have no right to—"

She spun. "My planet is facing annihilation."

His gaze went to her body, settling on the full curves of her breasts, perfectly outlined by her skintight suit. *Cren.* He jerked his gaze up.

"My entire species is facing destruction." Her eyes were hot and glowing. "With all your fancy technology and military might, you must know that. Yet, you refuse to help."

They stared at each other in the humming silence.

Agitated, she made an angry sound and turned back to the console, banging at the controls.

"Stop," he growled. "You'll wreck my ship."

"I'm trying to turn the damn autopilot off."

"Look, woman—"

She skewered him with a look. "My name is Eve. Sub-Captain Eve Traynor. Although since I'm a lowly Terran, you probably won't bother using it."

"Take me back to my ship."

"Negative."

"Woman." It ended with a growl.

"Just be quiet, War Commander. That will make this easier for both of us." She shot him a fake smile. "Or I'll gag you."

Fresh fury surged. This insolent female ignited his anger like nothing ever had before. Davion yanked on his hands and the restraints snapped. He unclipped his harness and rose.

Eve sprang to her feet. "Fuck."

He got a better look at her now. He could see every curve of her body, since it was covered in that slick fabric. She was strong and curvy. Eon females were larger, almost as tall and muscular as males. They also had limited curves and small breasts. He was distracted studying the Terran, so the kick she planted in his gut was deserved.

He staggered back and hit the chair.

She leaped at him, her knees hitting his chest. The momentum carried them over the chair to smack into the floor between the seats.

A wrestling match ensued, but Davion had the size advantage. An elbow connected with his jaw, but he managed to pin her beneath him. Her chest heaved, her eyes shooting lasers at him.

"What now, little Earth warrior?"

She bucked. Almost hard enough to dislodge him. He pressed down harder, giving her more of his weight. His hips settled between her thighs and Davion felt his own body responding.

By Alqin's axe. He was known for his absolute control in all things. And right now, it was missing.

She was warm and strong, and she smelled so damn good.

Blue eyes hit his and widened. Yes, it would be impossible for her to miss the fact that his erection was pressing against her belly.

Suddenly, alarms blared through the small cabin.

"What the hell?" she muttered.

Davion turned his head.

The shuttle's viewscreen was filled with the image of a Kantos ship.

Cren. He leaped to his feet, just as the Kantos ship opened fire.

THE SHUTTLE JOLTED. Eve jumped up beside the war commander. The ship jolted again, and it rocked so hard that she staggered and slammed into the warrior.

He grabbed her, righting her, then he dived for the controls.

Eve slid into the copilot's chair beside him. Damn, it was a large Kantos assault ship.

"I'm stabilizing the shuttle now." His tone was commanding, definitely "man in charge." "Check the shields."

Yes, sir. Her hands danced over the controls. "Already on it." Thankfully, the shuttle's systems seemed fairly straightforward. "Weapons?"

"Limited. We have a bank of lasers."

She worked through the controls. "Shields are damaged. Won't hold much longer." She swiped through, trying to find the weapons system.

Another barrage of Kantos fire hit them. The shuttle jerked and tilted. Sparks showered them from overhead.

Hell. Eve gripped the arm of her chair and gritted her teeth. Thann-Eon was cursing, but his hands were steady on the controls.

Eve found the weapons and fired up the lasers. He was right. They didn't have much fire power. Not against a fully-equipped Kantos cruiser. She took aim and let the lasers loose. Blue laser hit the Kantos ship.

The warrior turned, face set in hard lines. "I need my symbiont."

Eve's head jerked and she looked at his wrist. Access to his symbiont meant armor, weapons, increased strength.

"Eve."

They sustained another hit, and the ship tilted to the left. She got a glimpse of the planet looming ahead of them. They were racing toward it.

Another alarm sounded.

"Missiles have been locked on the shuttle," the computer said calmly. "Please take appropriate action."

"Missiles," Davion muttered.

Shit. "We—"

Boom.

The ship rattled so hard Eve's head was whipped from side to side. Then, she started floating up from her seat.

Dammit. The artificial gravity was gone.

She grabbed the armrest.

"Missile sheared off the back part of the engines," Thann-Eon barked.

Shit, shit. Eve snatched the antidote off her belt. She reached over, grabbed the warrior's thick wrist, and squeezed the injector. The orange fluid hit the black ooze and it dissolved instantly. "There you go, War Commander."

"At this juncture, I think you should call me Davion."

Oh, yeah, like they were best buds out for a little space adventure. She pulled herself back into her seat and strapped in. Davion yanked a harness across his chest and pressed a palm to the controls.

"Let's see what systems are still functioning," he said.

She heard him, but she was too busy watching as black scales flowed from the black wristband on his arm. The black flowed up, covering his forearm, his bicep. Then they flowed downward, covering his chest and legs. His face was impassive.

Holy hell. She watched, amazed. He was now almost fully encased in a black, scale-like armor. A few blue glints shone through in places.

The Kantos ship fired again.

"We've lost engines," Davion said. "I've only got docking thrusters."

Uh-oh. She touched her side of the console, but it was dead. "Can you send a mayday to your warship?"

"The comm system's been completely destroyed."

Great. Just great.

Davion pressed his palms to the controls and closed his eyes. Eve could see he was concentrating on something. The shuttle turned and she saw that he was using the thrusters to aim them directly at the planet below.

"What are you doing?" she asked.

"If we have any chance of survival, we need to land on the planet."

"You mean crash."

Black eyes, with those amazing, glowing, blue filaments met hers. "Yes. We need to crash land."

"Great, fucking great."

"Keep the Kantos off us."

"I'll pull out my full armament and do that."

He raised a brow. "Less sarcasm, more action, little warrior."

She shot him the finger. Then she leaned in close to him, tapping on his part of the console to get to the laser controls. She felt the heat radiating off him and ignored it. She took aim at the Kantos ship and fired. It was like using a slingshot against a lion.

"This Kantos ship have a weak spot?" she asked.

"What?" His face was strained. The planet was getting larger and larger.

"Does the Kantos ship have a weak spot?" she repeated.

"Small exhaust port directly under the back of the hull."

Okay. She could work with that. She swiveled the lasers, shifting to manual targeting. Then she bit off a curse. This wasn't going to be easy.

"That target area is too small," he said.

"Thanks for the pep talk. I feel better now."

"You are an infuriating woman."

"I get that a lot."

"You'll never hit it," he said.

"Watch me." She aimed and fired.

And missed.

Eve gritted her teeth, loosened her shoulders, took aim again, and fired.

"Are you always this stubborn?" Davion asked in a curious tone.

"Yes."

Gaze narrowed, she ignored him and fired again. This time she scored a direct hit—right on the exhaust port.

"Yes!" She threw her arms up.

The Kantos ship veered away. They'd sustained damage, and didn't want to risk another hit.

Davion blinked, staring at her.

Then, they hit the planet's atmosphere.

Oh, God.

The shuttle shuddered and rocked. It was like a roller-coaster—but not a fun one. More like one that made you throw up. They didn't have engines, so maneuvering was next to impossible. There was no way Davion could bring them in at the right angle. The shuttle vibrated. Hard. Something broke free behind her, and as it flew over her head, she ducked. It smacked against the viewscreen.

"Warrior—"

"All the systems are compromised." His voice was strained.

"Spell it out for me."

"It's going to be rough."

"So we're fucked. In the totally un-fun way."

"Quit talking and help me."

"Quit tossing orders around."

But both of them touched the controls, fighting to get what they could from the ailing shuttle's systems. Eve glanced at him. It was clear just how much the Eon warrior was doing to keep them from spiraling out of control. That hard jaw was clenched tight, and a bead of sweat rolled down his temple. It was purely him and his interaction with the computer that was keeping them relatively stable.

They rushed through huge, white fluffy clouds.

Below, dense jungle spread out before them in an ocean of green. The ship tilted wildly.

"We're coming in too fast!" she cried.

Davion gritted his teeth. "I'm trying to slow us down."

"Oh, fuck." Eve braced her hands on the console.

The trees rushed up at them. They were going to crash. Really badly.

She heard a click. He'd unclipped his harness. "What are you—?"

His heavy weight landed on her. He curled around her, pinning her to her seat.

Impact.

Crunching, smashing, breaking. Noise, a swirl of black and gray, pain.

Eve's last thought was that Davion was shielding her. Protecting her.

Then there was nothing.

CHAPTER FIVE

With a groan, Davion lifted his head. His vision was blurry, and it took a few seconds until it resolved.

He was in his shuttle. Or what was left of it. Eve was slumped beneath him, unconscious.

He pressed a finger to her neck and felt the tick of a strong pulse. He released a breath.

Her face was turned away from him, and with her out, he could finally take a chance to study her in better detail. She had a smattering of darker spots on her nose which he found intriguing, and long, inky black lashes.

She was also the most infuriating woman he'd ever met. He couldn't believe that she'd succeeded in abducting him off his warship.

Moving cautiously, Davion rose. He had a few bumps and bruises, but nothing was broken. He felt a pulse from his helian. It was unharmed and already working to heal his injuries.

The same could not be said about his shuttle.

It was destroyed.

He leaned over the console and checked the shuttle's systems. Nothing. No comms. No power. No way to contact the *Desteron*.

He shifted, opening some panels in the side wall of the shuttle. First things, first. He grabbed some strong, flexible, metal ties, swiveled, and crouched beside his abductor. He quickly tied her wrists and divested her of her weapons.

Then he found his already stocked backpack. There was no civilization on Hunter7. It was solely a warrior against the elements, so they'd need supplies. He found a second backpack for Eve and added some essential gear.

"What the hell?" Eve sat up. She glared at her bound wrists, then she transferred her heated look to Davion.

"It seemed fair," he said.

Her gaze narrowed.

"Now…" He crouched in front of her. "You answer my questions."

"Screw you, War Commander."

He shook his head. "I want your full name and occupation. I assume you're Space Corps."

Her glare was hot enough to sear to the bone.

"Eve," he prompted.

"Sub-Captain Eve Traynor. *Former* Space Corps."

There was enough acid on the word for him to deduce there was a story. "Current occupation?"

She smiled, humorlessly. "Criminal. I've been in prison the last five months."

Davion was pretty good at reading people, and this

woman was no criminal. "Why?"

"Clearly, I broke the law." Her jaw worked.

He saw shadows shift in her eyes. His helian stirred. The symbiont could detect emotion. He touched her arm. "Eve."

She blew out a breath. "I was framed. I was forced to take the fall for a Kantos confrontation to save an incompetent idiot who'd messed up. He also happened to be my captain."

Davion shook his head. "Why was someone lacking in skills and experience captaining a ship?"

"Because humans aren't perfect warriors. We let emotions affect us, and sometimes, we make bad decisions."

"And now your people want me?"

"Apparently."

Davion read between the lines. "They offered you your freedom."

"Yes and no. They also threatened my sisters. And you know, dangled the destruction of billions of Terrans over my head."

He stared at her. Her sisters? He shook his head. "And you wonder why the Eon wanted nothing to do with Earth after first contact."

"Look, I don't—"

There was a rush of sound overhead. A ship.

Davion rushed to the cracked forward viewscreen and looked out. He couldn't see much, just dense jungle canopy.

"Untie me!" Eve barked.

Davion kept searching the wall of green above them.

There. He caught a glimpse of the ship circling above the trees. "It's the Kantos."

His thoughts churned. Why were the Kantos after him? They were inside Eon territory and had to know they were declaring war by attacking him.

"War Commander, fucking untie me."

He spun. "My name is Davion."

"There is no time for—"

"Say it."

Their gazes locked. *Cren*, she was stubborn. He could tell she wanted to disobey him.

And why did he find that just a little bit intriguing? *Probably because no one ever disobeys you.*

"Davion," she bit out.

"There. Not so hard."

"You are incredibly aggravating."

He melded with his symbiont, and a second later, a knife formed from the scales on his wrist. The blade glowed blue.

He saw her staring at it.

"Funny, I was thinking the same thing about you." He cut through the bindings, then shoved one of the backpacks at her. "Now, we have to go."

His blade melded away, and he grabbed a shirt from his bags and pulled it on.

"Where are—?"

He pulled his pack on. "No time. For now, you follow my orders."

She bad-temperedly shoved her arms through the straps of her backpack. "Men. All the same, regardless of species. Bossy."

She stabbed a finger at his chest, and Davion felt a strange, electric sizzle. She must have felt it too, because she snatched her hand back and scowled.

"For now, we get away from the Kantos," she said. "But I won't be following your orders, War Commander. I follow no one's orders."

He grabbed her wrist, and when she tried to tug away, he held her with ease. "It's Davion. Now, let's go. That's a request, not an order, but you'd better move. A Kantos kill squad will be here soon."

She yanked her hand free, spun, and stomped off the ruined shuttle.

Davion followed. Well, his vacation was off to an interesting start.

UGH, she hated the jungle. Sweat was dripping down into Eve's eyes, and her high-tech spacesuit was *not* designed for the intense humidity. The suit stuck to her skin everywhere.

Ahead of her, Davion slashed through the trees and vines with the cool-ass machete blade that he'd created from his symbiont. It was attached to his arm, like an extension of him.

The man looked like he was out for an afternoon stroll.

He had a shirt on now, at least. His distracting chest was covered, but his powerful arms were bare. The muscles in his arm bulged with each swing of his sword.

Tearing her gaze off his bronze skin, she looked at the

sword again. It glowed a brilliant blue, like the filaments in his eyes, and it looked damn sharp. She wanted to ask questions about his symbiont, but she doubted he'd answer them.

They heard the sound of a ship passing nearby and both froze. The Kantos were clearly still searching for them.

"Down," Davion barked.

They both crouched, staring up through the jungle canopy. The plant beside her had huge leaves, twice as big as she was. Nearby, dense vines covered the trees, and glowed neon-green, pink, and blue.

The sounds of the searching ship faded.

"Let's keep moving," he said.

"Where to?"

"There's a comm station about seven *milar* from here." He tilted one wrist to look at the small comp screen attached to it.

"This is an Eon planet?" she asked.

"Yes. Hunter7. It's a training planet for warriors."

They kept moving, keeping up their rapid pace through the jungle. Eve didn't complain. She wanted as much distance between them and the Kantos as possible.

One good thing about the Kantos attack was that it might just sweeten the Eon into helping Earth. She glanced at the war commander's broad back. Maybe.

Finally, Davion waved at her and they paused for a drink. She grabbed a container of water from her backpack and gulped some down eagerly.

Suddenly, noises came from behind them. Something crashing through the jungle.

They both turned, staring in the direction they'd come.

"An animal?" she asked.

"Perhaps."

Then she heard a distinctive clicking sound. She cursed. "No. Kantos."

The sounds of pursuit were getting louder.

"Go," Davion growled.

They moved fast. This time, the warrior didn't slash at the foliage. They couldn't risk leaving a trail.

Vines and leaves slapped at her, as they crashed through the undergrowth. They startled a small, furry creature. It had huge eyes, and hissed at them before it leaped up in the branches and scurried away.

They kept running, fighting their way through the vegetation. A vine tangled around Eve, tightening like a snake.

Shit. She shoved against it. Davion turned, grabbed it, and yanked it off her.

"Thanks."

Together, they leaped over the log of a fallen tree with purple bark. Suddenly, Davion halted and stiffened. He lifted his head, scanning the jungle.

"Davion?" she asked cautiously. She couldn't hear or see anything.

A Kantos bug leaped out of a tree, landing between them.

This particular alien had a sturdy, armored body with six legs, and long antennae on its round head. It also had two sharp mandible pincers, covered in serrated edges.

She'd seen this type of bug before. They were like Kantos scout dogs.

Davion engaged, moving so fast he was a blur. Black armor spilled out over his body, his blue sword extending out from his wrist.

As he crashed into the Kantos creature, Eve held her breath. They swiveled, and he slashed at the creature in a whirl of blue.

Damn, the man could fight.

She watched as the bug slammed Davion into a tree. She winced.

Then, she sensed movement behind her. Company.

Calm dropped over her, and she grabbed a neon-green vine hanging right beside her. It pulsed in her hand. She turned, and she and another ugly Kantos bug faced each other.

"Come on, you butt-ugly creepy-crawly."

The Kantos bug made a clicking sound, moving from side to side. A smell wafted from it, and Eve's stomach churned—rot and decay.

Suddenly, the bug launched at her.

Wait. Wait. Every instinct told her to move, but she held in place.

When the alien reached her, she jumped, and wrapped the vine around the bug's neck. She spun over its hard back, coiling the vine around it. As soon as her boots hit dirt, she pulled back.

The bug screeched and wriggled like crazy. Its legs scrabbled on the muddy ground as it tried to break free.

Eve gritted her teeth. *No, you damn well don't.* But the

creature was strong, and she couldn't hold it much longer. A second later, two strong arms wrapped around her from behind. Davion's hands closed on the vine, right beside hers. He added his strength to hers, and they yanked back, hard.

The Kantos bug's neck snapped.

As the alien's body dropped to the ground, Eve leaned over, sucking in air. She glanced over and saw the bug he'd been fighting was lying on the ground, not moving. Green blood leaked down its side.

Suddenly, Davion stiffened.

Two Kantos soldiers stepped out of the trees.

They walked on four long, jointed legs, had strong torsos of hard, brown shell, and two arms held out in front of them. The edges of their arms were razor-sharp. Kantos soldiers had no need for weapons when they had their own built in.

Hardened armored plates covered their shoulders and the top of their heads. Four small, yellow eyes glowed in two rows of two above a narrow mouth filled with very sharp teeth.

Fuck.

The Kantos soldiers rushed forward. Eve and Davion burst into action. *Kick. Duck. Punch. Spin.*

Davion was a fierce haze of black. Eve rammed a boot into the gut of her soldier and watched him stumble. He snarled at her. Damn, they were ugly.

She spun and jumped, her roundhouse catching him in his nasty face. He staggered back.

"Warrior." She rammed into the soldier, sending it slamming into Davion's opponent.

Anticipating her move, Davion dropped, slashing out

with his deadly blue sword. His soldier was cut almost in two. With a wild clicking noise, it made a kamikaze charge at Davion.

Eve's soldier leaped back. His burning, yellow eyes fell on her, deciding she was the weaker prey. She smiled wickedly. "Bring it, bug boy."

The soldier threw out its sharp, sword-like arms. He came at her, slashing.

Shit. Eve snatched a branch off the ground and swung it up like a bat. It smacked into the soldier's arms and she heard him grunt.

"How do you like that?" she yelled.

She swung again, hitting the Kantos' chest. It screeched.

"Oh yeah, I have more where that came from, Mr. Creepy."

He rushed her on those fast-moving legs and she tried to twist away, but she felt a burn on her thigh.

Ow. She tried to block the pain, but as she turned, her leg muscle spasmed and she stumbled. The soldier tackled her, and they crashed into the rotting leaves in a tangle of limbs.

The Kantos rose up above her and she kicked her legs, trying to get him off her. "Oh, you like to get up close and personal? Well, just because you're bigger doesn't mean you're tougher than me, asshole."

He raised his clawed hand.

Eve's muscles bunched, and she readied herself to dodge and knock him off her—

Suddenly, the tip of a blue sword burst through the soldier's chest, just inches from her eyes.

She saw the Kantos' four beady little eyes flare. Davion ripped his sword free and the Kantos collapsed. Eve quickly rammed her arms up and shoved the soldier off her.

"Jeez." She pulled in some deep breaths. "They always smell so bad."

Davion looked down at her. "Do you always talk so much when you fight?"

"Depends on my mood."

He gave a tiny shake of his head, and Eve thought that perhaps he was amused.

"You are a decent fighter, Sub-Captain."

"Ooh, big praise." She shrugged. "Since we encountered the Kantos, we've adapted our fight training. Projectiles don't always work on their hard bodies, so we learn a lot more hand-to-hand, and sword fighting."

"Industrious." He held out a hand and she took it. He pulled her up.

They stared at each other. Her blood was fired up, pumping thickly through her veins. They'd just taken down two Kantos bugs and two soldiers. Where Davion held her fingers, she felt that weird, tantalizing tingle.

Then they both moved closer to each other, their chests bumping.

She felt the air around him charge and heat. Oh God, it was like hot, edgy desire was wrapping around her like smoke.

"Oh, shit," she said.

"Indeed."

She had no idea if she kissed him or if he kissed her, but suddenly her arms wrapped around him and he scooped her off her feet. Eve was crushed against his hard chest, the kiss rough and hungry and fierce.

God, the man tasted like nothing she'd ever sampled before. A drug she wanted more of. She moaned. His fingers bit into her ass, while his other hand slid into her hair, tugging her head back. His kiss deepened, his tongue sliding into her mouth.

Eve bit his lip and tasted blood in her mouth. He growled and tugged on her hair. She wanted to devour him, be devoured.

Somewhere close by, an animal howled.

They released each other and stumbled back. Davion reached up and touched his lip. Eve licked hers.

Shit. Damn. Fuck.

What the *hell* was that?

Davion straightened, slamming down on the emotion soaking the air. With it gone, Eve felt a little bereft.

His face was unreadable, even if his eyes looked a little clouded. "We have to go."

Eve nodded, skimming her hands down her suit.

"You aren't injured?" he asked.

"Slight graze on my thigh. It's fine." Blocking out all her thoughts, she leaned down, and gripped one of the downed Kantos' arms. She pressed a boot to his jointed elbow and yanked. The forearm broke off and she held it up. Makeshift sword. She swung it in a test swing and nodded. It would do.

Davion stared at her for a moment. Then he pulled out her blaster. "You might need this as well."

"Thanks." She slipped it into her holster. Then she hefted her new weapon and nodded. "Now, let's move."

CHAPTER SIX

Davion moved fast through the giant plants, Eve keeping pace beside him. The little Terran kept surprising him.

In the distance, the call of some sort of beast echoed. He cocked his head. Far enough away to not worry about.

He pulled in a deep breath, savoring the fresh air. Despite the circumstances, it was always nice to be off the ship and not breathing recycled air. He breathed again, and this time his symbiont-enhanced senses brought him Eve's scent.

She was perspiring, they both were, but he could easily pull the thread of her own unique scent from beneath it. Something flared in his body.

Davion could still taste her as well.

He shook his head. He needed an attraction to the kidnapping Terran criminal like he needed a Kantos kill squad to jump out of the sky and land on top of him.

Davion tilted his wrist, checking the timer on his

comp screen. They still had a bit of time before he estimated the next biome shift would hit. Though Hunter7 was designed to be unpredictable and keep a warrior guessing, so it was possible his estimate could be off.

He heard a low curse and glanced back.

His Terran had slowed, lifting her boots up through a patch of sticky mud.

"Keep moving, Eve. We want to get to that comm station sooner, rather than later."

She shot him a look and another curse.

Shaking his head, and ignoring the unfamiliar urge to smile, he pushed some huge leaves aside. On the other side was a small clearing, ringed by multicolored vegetation. The trees here speared high into the sky, their trunks virulent pink with leaves a wild mix of blue, green, and yellow.

"Wow." Eve tipped her head back, mouth open.

Davion's gaze stayed on her. He studied her surprisingly full lips, then the long column of her throat. For a second, he relived the kiss—the searing passion and heated need.

She had an elegant neck, long and slim, yet she was so tough. Her body was lean muscle and strength, but it was easy to glimpse the femininity beneath it.

Eve's hair barely reached her shoulders, and it was a gorgeous, fascinating black. It matched her dark spacesuit that was built for stealth. A suit that also showed her curves.

He blew out a breath. He'd never seen a more enticing female.

His cock stirred. Okay, it wasn't just her looks.

Perhaps he enjoyed their verbal sparring, and watching her fight had something to do with the attraction as well. Eon females could be warriors, but few chose that as a profession.

Lost in thought, he didn't pay any attention as Eve wandered closer to one of the colorful trees. It was covered in bright-yellow pods.

She reached up.

Davion snapped out of his reverie. "Eve, no—"

Poof.

The small pods on the tree burst, a pink mist pumping into the air. The small particles hung for a second, and Eve laughed, waving her hand through it.

Davion's chest contracted. "Eve!"

As soon as her fingers touched the mist, it started to stir. It swirled around her body, moving like it was caught by a strong wind.

"What the hell?" Eve stiffened.

The mist solidified and clamped down on her body. The pink substance stuck to her, trapping her arms to her sides. A line of it ran back into the tree like a vine.

"Fucking hell." She started to struggle.

"Hold still." Davion hurried over. "The more you move, the more it will tighten."

The substance contracted, lifting her off the ground. She swung from the tree, her feet well-clear of the ground.

She stilled instantly, her eyes wide. "What is it?"

"Most things on this planet are designed to entrap and kill you." They were at eye level.

She hissed.

Davion called on his symbiont and generated a knife. He saw her eyes flash as he lifted the blade to her chest. He started cutting into the sticky, pink substance.

"Hold still," he warned.

"Where do you think I'm going to go?" she said dryly.

"Are you always this ornery?"

She tilted her head. "When trapped by strange alien bubble gum that's trying to strangle me? Yes. Actually, most of the time."

He grunted, getting one of her arms free.

"So, what exactly is this place, again?" she asked.

"Hunter7 is designed to test an Eon warrior. To push him to his limits."

"Great. And this is where you chose to have your vacation?"

"Yes."

She snorted. "Why am I not surprised?"

Davion finally managed to free her, and she dropped down from the tree. He caught her as she fell.

They stared at each other for a charged second, and his gaze dropped to her lips. Again, he remembered that kiss.

Eve quickly shifted, twisting to get her feet on the ground. But before he let her go, he detected her pulse jumping in her throat.

She stomped across the small clearing. "Right. Don't touch any pretty plants. Everything is out to kill you. Lesson learned."

She was putting space between them. For some reason, Davion found it very satisfying to know his presence affected her.

He nodded, his knife melting away. He moved up beside her. "Let's keep moving. I highly doubt the Kantos will give up this easily."

Her blue gaze flicked to him. "You think they're hunting us?"

"For sure."

"Why?"

Davion frowned. "I'd like to know."

"Well, they don't know I'm here, so they must be after you."

"It seems I'm a popular man."

"I assume you didn't broadcast your plans to vacation here."

"No, but it wasn't a secret either. It's possible the Kantos intercepted a communication."

They pushed through the next wall of vegetation and kept hiking through the jungle. Without much conversation, they trekked on for another hour, pausing briefly every once in a while to listen for any approaching threats. The plant life got thicker, and he once again used his sword to slash a path for them. Then the sound of water caught his ears.

When he stepped out of the trees this time, there was a large chasm cutting through the ground ahead of them. It was like a giant gash in the ground. He peered down at the river raging below, heaving and rushing over sharp rocks.

Eve groaned. "Please tell me we don't have to cross this." She wiped an arm across her forehead, mopping off her sweat-dampened face.

"The comm station is on that hill." He pointed to the peak across the river.

She groaned again.

"Come on, Terran. Surely you enjoy a challenge."

She made a gesture with her hand, her middle finger raised. He didn't know exactly what it meant, but he could guess.

Davion scanned the area, and spotted some sturdy, long vines dangling from the nearby trees. He grabbed one, testing it. Then he looked down at the water.

"Here." He passed one vine to her.

She took it, tugging on it. Her lips tipped up. "Me Tarzan, you Jane."

He frowned. He had no idea what she was talking about. "What?"

"Nothing. Okay, time for a little swing." She winked. "See you on the other side, warrior."

She pushed off. Of course, she did. There was no caution or hesitation in this woman. She barreled into any situation with a confidence he admired.

She swung out powerfully and he watched her arch through the air. She was such a surprise, this Terran warrior.

All of a sudden, there was a violent splash of water.

Davion took a step forward. *No.* His muscles locked.

A giant, streamlined, reptilian creature lunged up from the water. Its giant, fang-filled jaws were opening... and aimed right at Eve.

FUCKING *FUCK*.

One second, Eve was enjoying the wind in her face as she swung over the river, the next she was watching a freaking enormous, crocodile-like monster rear up out of the water.

Shit.

It looked hungry, and she was clearly the snack on offer.

She pulled her legs up. There was nowhere to go, and the thing was *huge*. It looked like some sort of dinosaur had mated with a crocodile and given birth to this mutant offspring.

Oh, God, all those teeth...

She cursed the Eon warriors and their need to have this deadly, everything-out-to-kill-you planet.

The beast was coming up beneath her, moving fast. Her pulse hammered under her skin, and her heart felt like it was about to tear out of her chest.

Suddenly, a heavy weight hit her from behind. Large arms clamped around her, and they swung forward with a sharp jerk. The giant reptile snapped its jaws closed, inches behind them.

Davion's arms held her tight as they swung the rest of the way to the other side of the chasm.

They hit the ground together, releasing the vines, and both of them rolling to their knees. Eve turned, watching the giant dino-croc sink back into the water.

"Damn. Damn." She tried to calm her breathing.

"You okay?" Davion asked.

"Yes. No. Jeez." She looked at him. "I hate your planet."

He smiled.

It made an already attractive face damn irresistible. He was so damn big, strong, and powerful. And he'd saved her life.

Eve pulled in another breath, adrenaline surging through her veins. She was alive and free. They were both gloriously alive.

She crawled toward him.

He watched her come, his face impassive.

She pressed her hands to his chest and he fell back. She straddled his lap.

Her mouth hit his.

This time, the kiss shot straight to wild in seconds. Eve opened her lips and his tongue surged into her mouth. She ground against him, and his hands clamped on her ass, pulling her closer. She felt the very large bulge between her thighs and undulated against it. His tongue stroked hers, and she sucked on it, kissing him harder. Then his hands were tearing at her suit.

She showed him the release near her neck, and he pushed it down. The suit spilled open, baring her breasts. Support was built into the suit, so no bra was required. He had instant full access to her naked breasts.

He made a hungry sound and his mouth closed over one nipple.

Oh God. Her head dropped back. He sucked hard and she moaned. Pleasure arrowed through her, right to her middle. Hungrily, his mouth moved to the other breast, and she tangled her hands in his thick hair.

"Beautiful." He murmured the word against her skin.

His hands bit into her, and she felt the desire pulsing off him.

He made her feel beautiful.

Then, a vicious squawk echoed overhead, and they froze.

Whoa. What the hell was she doing? Eve leaped up, pulling her suit closed. Her damn hands weren't steady and it took a few tries.

Davion rose stiffly, and she could hardly miss the giant bulge in the front of his pants.

"Maybe something on this planet is affecting us?" she said. "A pollen, or pheromone, or something."

His brow was scrunched and he didn't look convinced. "That must be it."

"You're Eon and I'm Terran."

"I'm well aware. I'm a war commander, and you're a Terran criminal."

Eve shoved her hands through her hair. The Kantos were hunting them, she'd almost gotten eaten by a tree and a dino-croc, and now she was making out with the Eon war commander that she'd abducted.

A fierce, annoying, Eon war commander.

She was clearly losing her mind.

"We need to get to the comm station," he said. "That is our only goal. I never, ever get sidetracked by anything."

Right, so kissing her was a mistake. "Never?"

"Never."

"Don't you ever take a day for yourself? Chill out? Relax?"

His brow creased, like she'd asked him if he liked to salsa dance naked on his bridge. "No."

Eve smoothed her hands down her thighs. "War commanders aren't allowed to have fun, huh?"

His gaze had dropped to follow her hands, then he jerked it up. "My life is my job. I get pleasure from serving the Eon Empire."

"That sounds uptight and lame."

His eyes flashed. "I'd expect that response from a Terran."

She rolled her eyes at him. "Everyone is entitled to do some things for themselves, Davion. Even you."

He looked unconvinced.

Moving on. "So, the plants are trying to kill us, the animals are trying to kill us—"

"I warned you that everything on Hunter7 is designed to test you."

Just great. "And the Kantos are trying to kill us." She sucked in a deep breath. Time to get her head back in the game. "Where's the comm station?"

Davion lifted his head, looking at a distant hill. "Up there."

Eve set her shoulders back, then scowled. "I lost my Kantos weapon in the river." She hoped the dino-croc choked on it. "I still have my blaster but a sword would be better."

"There are weapons caches all over the planet. We'll pass one on the way to the comm station. We can do better than a piece of Kantos arm."

Weapons caches. Of course there were.

Davion gave her one of his unreadable looks and then

spun, trekking off into the jungle. She followed, trying not to look at his ass. Again, she remembered the very large cock brushing between her legs.

She swallowed a groan. Yep, definitely losing her mind.

They trekked in silence for a while, and were getting closer to the hill, when the ground started shaking.

Davion cursed.

"What now?" Eve held her arms out to keep her balance.

"I was hoping we'd make it to the comm station before this."

"This?" She grabbed his arm. "What is *this*?"

The ground tilted and split open nearby. She sucked in a breath.

"The biome is changing."

It was what? Sand began to spill out of the crack, and she watched the jungle vegetation nearby start shrinking, like it had been subjected to heat.

Davion grabbed her, holding on tight as the ground continued to shake around them. A tree toppled, crashing to the ground. Sand rose up, covering it.

Eve held onto Davion, watching more sand wash over their boots. A few minutes later, the shaking stopped.

Eve looked around and gasped. *Holy space dust.* The jungle was…gone.

The air was dry and the sun felt extra hot on her skin. All around them lay huge desert sand dunes.

"Davion…"

"Hunter7 is a synthetic planet, Eve."

She stared up at him. "You made it?"

He nodded. "We used a proto-planet, and our scientists augmented it. It was designed to be a proving ground for our warriors. Every few hours, the biome changes. A new climate, new vegetation, new animals, new challenges."

"All out to kill you."

"To test you."

She snorted. "And the comm station?"

"Still in place. As are the weapons caches, healing stations, and rest stations. They're scattered around to aid warriors."

Eve shook her head. "It's like being in a giant videogame." She tipped her head. "How are the stations restocked?"

"It's all automatically done by the planet. When a biome changes, the stations are replenished according to the program."

"And the dead Kantos and your shuttle?"

"Dead organic matter is absorbed by the planet. Inorganic materials, including objects like shuttles, are left untouched."

"What if a warrior is badly injured or killed?"

"Then he's failed the test of his abilities. However, warriors in training who are sent to the hunter planets are monitored and retrieved, if necessary." Davion searched the dunes. "There."

She followed the direction he pointed, and saw a glint of sunlight off metal at the peak of a huge dune.

The comm station.

She smiled briefly. Not too far away. "Okay, let's go

before giant sand creatures try to eat us, or something worse happens."

He shook his head, and she was pretty sure he was trying not to smile. They started trudging through the sand.

There was a roar of sound in the sky.

They both looked up. Two Kantos ships—that looked like ugly flying insects—cut through the blue, heading toward them.

Davion cursed and Eve closed her eyes. It looked like she'd jinxed them.

"There's no cover." He gripped her arm. "Run!"

CHAPTER SEVEN

They sprinted up a dune. It was slow going. The sand certainly wasn't making it easy.

Laser fire struck the ground nearby and Davion leaped, taking Eve with him. They hit the top of the dune, somersaulted, then started rolling down the other side.

Cren.

Eve came up cursing, spitting sand out of her mouth.

They ran, hearing the Kantos ships circling. Eve yanked out her laser weapon and was taking shots at the ships. Ahead, at the peak of the next dune, Davion could see the outline of the comm station.

So close.

A Kantos ship cut through the sky in front of them. Davion melded with his helian, and the weapon on his arm morphed into a blaster. He aimed up at the ship and fired.

Boom.

It only took one shot. The laser blast hit the ship, and it exploded in a fireball of flames and smoke. It crashed into the sand nearby.

"Move," he barked.

"I'm moving," she snapped back.

They both pumped their arms as they dashed up the final dune. They just had to get a message off to the *Desteron,* and help would be sent.

The second Kantos ship roared overhead. This one was bigger.

Boom. Boom.

A barrage of laser fire blasted the comm station.

The installation exploded, rattling the ground beneath Davion and Eve. Eve jerked and started to slip back down the dune. Davion grabbed her.

She stared up at the destroyed station, her mouth open.

There was another bombardment of laser fire. It hit the sand not far from them, tracking toward them. Davion slammed into Eve.

Out of the corner of his eye, he saw the red flames of the comm station suck inward. *Cren.* He knew what was about to happen.

He covered Eve's body and they slid down the dune. As they slowed, he pressed her into the sand.

The massive explosion was deafening, turning the world a brilliant white. Something heavy slammed into his back, and he heard the whine of the Kantos ship's engines as it sped out of the blast zone.

Eve shifted under him.

"Hold still," he warned. "They used plasma weapons. And they'll be back."

They stayed there, partly buried by the sand. Davion's ears were ringing. Sure enough, the ship circled overhead again, clearly searching for them.

Or their dead bodies.

The minutes ticked by, and finally, the ship sped off.

Davion sat up and pulled Eve up beside him. She pushed her tangled hair out of her face, sand streaming out of it. Her face was covered in grit and grime.

She shook her head, fingers rubbing her ears, and stared at the ruins of the comm station. "Well, fuck."

He rose and she pushed to her feet beside him. He glanced down at himself, and saw that he was coated in dust and grime as well.

"And I lost my favorite blaster." Her nose screwed up. "Is there another comm station?"

He nodded.

Her nose wrinkled more. "Your face tells me you aren't too happy about something, warrior. I can feel unhappiness pumping off you."

His people had told him before that his face was like stone—scary and unreadable. And he'd spent years learning to stop his helian-amplified emotions from leaking out. That she could read him so easily was slightly disturbing. "My helian magnifies my emotions."

Her eyes turned curious, dropping to his wrist. "Really?"

"A warrior usually can shut it off."

She made a sound. "You don't. It blasts off you like a wave."

"Not usually."

Eve nodded. "Well, this fucked up situation would be enough to make anyone gush pissed-off vibes."

Davion didn't think it was simply the situation, it was this woman as well.

"So, the other comm station," she prompted.

"It's a day's trek away," he told her.

She groaned. "And in the meantime, the planet will keep changing and trying to kill us."

He nodded.

"And the Kantos will keep hunting us." She cocked her head. "They want you badly."

"I noticed," he said dryly.

"Why?"

"I'm a war commander in the Eon Fleet, Eve." His pointed gaze zeroed in on her face. "A lot of people are interested in abducting me."

She smiled. "Touché."

"I don't know what that means."

"Good point." She rubbed a hand down her face, smearing the dirt on it.

Davion was well aware they were both battered and tired. They needed to rest and refuel before they pushed on to the next comm station. He tugged off his backpack and offered her some water.

She wasted no time chugging it back. He sipped his water and pulled out some nutrition bars. He handed her one and tore open his own.

Taking a big bite, she paused and chewed. "This tastes *way* better than the crap Space Corps gives us for missions."

He almost smiled. "I didn't pack much. I had planned to hunt fresh food." He glanced at his wrist. "There should be a healing station close by." He spotted the glowing dot on his screen. "It isn't too far. It will have additional food, water, and medical supplies."

"Okay." She nodded. "That's something."

"Also, the biome doesn't change at night."

"Well, that's good, too." She smiled.

Davion couldn't believe she could smile at a time like this. He nodded in the direction of the healing station, and they started trudging through the sand.

The sun was scorching hot and unforgiving. It was enough to make him wish he had chosen the pleasure planet option for his vacation.

Then he glanced at Eve. Fascinating, intriguing, infuriating Eve.

Maybe not.

They continued on over the dunes, the ground becoming stony. Small, sharp rocks poked up through the sand in places.

"The station should be close," he said.

"Thank God."

Davion stopped, looked at his wrist screen again. Eve took a few more steps, glancing out toward the horizon.

Suddenly, the ground shifted beneath their feet, the sand rippling.

They both froze.

"Biome change?" Eve said.

He frowned. "Too soon."

Then, Eve's boots started sinking into the sand. "What the—?"

Davion started sinking as well.

"Quicksand." Eve threw her hands in the air. "Just what we needed."

They sank fast, the sand sucking at their legs. Davion tried to lift his boots up, but the sand was too viscous.

"Don't struggle," he warned. "You'll just sink faster."

"Have I told you that I hate this planet?"

By Eshar's bow, she made him want to laugh at the worst times.

Davion was waist-deep now. He made swimming motions, trying to get closer to her.

"Eve, take my hand." He stretched out one arm.

She reached out, their fingers brushing. They missed.

They were sinking fast now. Davion kicked his legs, trying to keep his head above the thick, sticky sand. Every move felt like it was draining his energy. Soon, only the tops of their heads were sticking up out of the quicksand.

"Dammit." Eve was panting from the exertion of stopping herself from sinking.

Davion lunged at her and their hands gripped. He tugged her closer, sliding an arm around her. Sand filled her mouth and she spat it out.

"Hope you have a plan, warrior," she gasped.

He called on his symbiont and generated a rope. It coiled on his arm and he threw it hard, tossing it toward the closest rock.

The blue rope slithered around the rock, forming a loop.

"Nice work." She grinned at him. And for a moment, he was distracted.

That smile lit up her face, smoothing some of the

hard edges life had put on her features. Keeping his arm tight around her, he heaved on the rope.

His muscles strained. Gritting his teeth, he pulled them slowly toward the side, his muscles trembling with the effort. When they were close enough, he shoved her toward the edge.

"Go, Eve."

Her face set, she gripped the rope. He heaved her toward it and she climbed along it, finally pulling herself over the edge of the quicksand and onto firm ground.

Davion sank deeper into the sand. His muscles burned, and tiredness washed over him.

"Come on, warrior."

Eve stood, planted her feet, and gripped the rope. She started pulling on it, reeling him in to the side.

A moment later, Davion dredged up enough energy to drag himself out. They both collapsed on the firm sand.

"Thanks," he said.

"You, too."

He wanted to do nothing more than lie there and rest, but it wasn't safe. "Come on. The healing station is close."

"Right. Just as long as sand monsters or some other nasty thing doesn't eat us before then."

His lips twitched.

She smiled. "I saw that, mighty War Commander Thann-Eon. You almost laughed."

"Come on, Earth warrior."

Staggering together, arms around each other, they managed to get upright and headed in the right direction.

They circled around another dune and Eve gave an excited cry.

Davion lifted his head, and spotted the tiny pool of water with a tree beside it.

"Oasis." Eve rushed forward toward it, but she'd clearly learned. She stopped well back from the water's edge, staring into the cool, blue-green pond.

"Is it safe?" she asked. "The water isn't poisonous, or home to flesh-eating aliens, or something?"

He looked at his screen, running a quick scan. Now, he smiled. "The water is safe."

"Race you, warrior." She broke into a sprint.

A second later, Davion found himself following her across the sand. As they got closer to the small pool, Eve began to strip off her suit.

By Ston's sword. His steps faltered. She shed the suit, near naked as she closed the distance to the water. She was all long, golden limbs and slender curves. And a strength that was all too irresistible.

He watched her race into the water, splashing and laughing.

He couldn't breathe.

EVE WAS happy as hell to get her suit off. She stood up in the water, splashing it against her. She was clad only in simple black panties, and as the cool, refreshing water slid over her, she moaned. It was so good.

"Get in here, warrior." She splashed more water on her neck and turned her head.

Oh. Oh, hell.

Davion had retracted his armor and pulled his shirt off. His gaze was on her, though. His face was unreadable as always, but his gaze was burning hot. It dipped down to her bare breasts.

Okay, maybe in her mad rush to get clean and cool, she hadn't thought this all through.

Then she got distracted. His hands were at the fastenings of his trousers.

She swallowed. Her gaze moved over him, down his muscled chest, his unbelievable abs. Heat flaring in her cheeks, she ducked down into the water.

Jeez, Eve. She felt like a damn teenager. *Don't lust after the alien war commander you abducted.* Repeat. *Don't lust after the alien war commander you abducted.*

She rose out of the water, careful to keep one arm crossed over her chest. Of course, she couldn't stop herself from looking at him again. He was partly turned away from her, and this time she took in the expanse of bronze skin and the hard muscles of his back. He had a few intriguing scars, as well.

The man was unreal. Built like a dream. Or a dark, dirty fantasy.

And now, all he was wearing was tight, black, boxer-style underwear. *Shit.*

She dropped back into the water and floated onto her back. She was clean and alive. She needed to focus on that.

Davion moved into the water and she heard him splashing. She also imagined him washing that huge, muscular body of his. They stayed silent, floating together in the pool.

"I'd hoped to have the chance to swim while I was here," he murmured.

Eve turned her head. "A nice change from misty, starship showers."

"Exactly."

"So you *sometimes* do things for pleasure."

His gaze met hers. "Sometimes."

She swallowed. "Well, we have a saying on Earth. All work and no play makes Jack a dull boy. Or in this case, Davion a dull boy."

"My work is important and keeps me busy."

She made a scoffing sound.

"Warriors enter the Military Academy at ten. I was raised to protect my empire and its people."

She rolled in the water. "Ten? You start your training so young?"

"Yes," he said. "Do you take time off?"

"Okay, well, not a lot." And she'd had nothing but time the last five months.

"I didn't think so." His tone was dry.

She moved her hands through the water. "But when I do, I visit with my sisters on Earth. One lives in Tokyo, in a country called Japan. I love the place. It's where my grandmother came from." Eve had loved her Grandmother Kimiko so damn much. She'd loved to tell the story about how she'd fallen in love with a handsome American soldier and had Eve's mother.

"And when I have time off, I come to hunter planets like this one."

Eve rolled her eyes. "You need lessons on what relaxing means, warrior."

"Hungry?" Davion asked.

"Starving."

She heard him move toward the edge and, with a shaky sigh, she followed.

Water dripping down his skin, he moved to a solid, dome-shaped, metal box resting at the base of the tree. He pressed his palm against it and it slid open with a hiss.

Inside was food, water, and supplies. He handed her some soft fabric—an Eon-sized shirt, she realized—and she used it to dry off, before she slipped it on. Next, he handed her some small packages.

"Energy-rich nutrition packs. I can't promise they'll taste that great to a Terran palate."

Eve tore the first packet open. "I don't care if it tastes like dust, I'm starving."

She took a bite. Then she paused. "Oh, my God." The stuff tasted amazing. Even better than the bar he'd given her earlier. It was rich, smooth, and sweet. "This is the greatest thing I've ever tasted!"

As she munched on it, she surreptitiously watched Davion pull on some clean clothes. They looked almost identical to the ones he'd been wearing. Clearly, high fashion wasn't a thing in the Eon military.

"So, what's the plan?" she asked.

He sat, opening his own pack of food. "We head for the next comm station. Make it as far as we can before nightfall. If we can make it to a rest station for the night, it would be best. It will have safe shelter. Otherwise, we'll need to find our own shelter."

She nodded. "How long until the biome changes again?"

"My best guess is a few hours. Before nightfall, but it's set to be unpredictable."

They ate in companionable silence. The desert heat soon had them dry, and Eve was almost sorry to slide back into her spacesuit. But she knew the suit would give her more protection from the elements and any surprise attacks.

They packed the food into their backpacks. Davion handed her an Eon blaster, and showed her how to use it. She also took a small, ornate blade out of the healing station.

"That's it?" she asked.

"Until we find a weapons cache."

She slid the heavy Eon blaster into the holster where her StrikeFire blaster usually sat. She thought longingly of her weapon, lost back near the ruined comm station. She sheathed the knife on her belt.

It was time to head off. A part of Eve didn't want to leave the tiny oasis. It was like a little calm in the storm.

But before she knew it, they were trudging through the sand again, scanning the skies for the Kantos.

And the ground for any new hazards.

"You really put all your warriors through this?" She studied his rugged face.

"Yes."

"I can't believe this planet is synthetic." She hated the place, but it was still amazing. "It can make any sort of biome or surroundings?"

"Yes."

"Amazing." The Space Corps had synthesizers on the fleet's ships—to make food, parts, clothes. The devices had started their lives as 3D printers on Earth years ago, used to make simple parts and tools. But over time, the technology had increased and improved so they could make just about anything. Still, the Eon had outdone them. This entire planet was a giant synthesizer on steroids.

Within another hour, they were both hot and sweaty again. Yep, Eve hated this planet with the heat of a thousand burning suns. She paused to shift the backpack on her shoulders, and saw something move in the sand.

With a shriek, she jerked back. "Snake!" She launched herself into Davion's arms.

The scaly, sinuous creature hissed, half buried in the sand. It shot her what appeared to be an indignant look, then slithered off.

"You're afraid of snakes?" Davion's eyebrows rose and his arms tightened on her.

"Yes."

"You'll dive into a fight with the Kantos without blinking, you'll sneak onto a heavily-armed Eon warship and abduct a war commander, but you're afraid of a small animal?"

She sniffed and wriggled until he let her down. "A slithery, icky, and no-doubt poisonous animal."

This time, Davion laughed. He threw his handsome head back, and laughed hard. It was a gorgeous sound, and Eve found herself staring at him, drinking him in.

Shaking his head, he nudged her onward.

Well, she was glad she could provide him with some comic relief. "So, you were supposed to have a week off?"

"My first in a long time."

She felt a smidge of remorse. "Well, sorry about messing that up. You know, if the fate of an entire planet wasn't on the line, we wouldn't have kidnapped you."

He turned his head. "But it isn't just about your planet, is it? Your sisters?"

She nodded. "Lara and Wren. Do you have siblings?"

Davion shook his head. "Procreation is the field of Eon scientists. They select genetic material from the healthiest, smartest Eon. Children are assigned to Eon who apply to start families. My parents only selected me."

"Seriously? You make super babies and people adopt them."

"Yes. Eon fertility is a tricky thing. Our helian regulates it, and only mated pairs are fertile. But over the last few decades, the rate of mating has dropped, and so natural conception has declined."

"Hmm. Any idea why?"

He shook his head. "To combat the problem, the scientists started the breeding program. In fact, my parents are key Eon scientists."

"Science for the win. Is that why you warriors all look so similar?"

"Partly. There is more diversity in the regular Eon population, but the dominant features that make a good warrior means most warriors look alike." He paused. "Do you look like your sisters?"

"Yep. My older sister Lara and I could be twins. My

younger sister Wren has curly hair and way more curves, which she complains about a lot."

"You're close to your sisters."

"Yes. They drive me crazy sometimes, but I love them."

"Your parents?"

Eve tried not to stiffen. "My father is dead."

"I'm sorry."

"It was in an early confrontation with the Kantos."

"The Kantos have spilled a lot of blood." He paused. "And your mother?"

Eve pulled in a breath. "Isn't really worthy of the title. She kind of lost it after my father died."

"She didn't care for you and your sisters?" he asked quietly.

"No. She lost herself in a bottle. The last thing she said to me was in a message, telling me I was a disgrace." Eve shook her head at the old anger. Her mom had never taken the time to ask Eve what the hell had happened. This was a topic she *really* didn't want to discuss. "You said the Kantos have spilled a lot of blood. And they want more. You're okay with them annihilating Earth?"

"I never said that."

Eve saw the sympathy on his face. She nodded. "But you don't speak for all of the Eon. It was your king who declared that there would be no contact with Earth."

"We have a new king now."

"Really?" She hadn't known that. This could be a good thing.

"And you snuck onto his warship and abducted his war commander."

Eve wrinkled her nose. "Not by choice." Okay, maybe the new king wasn't going to be a huge fan. "So, tell me about the Eon homeworlds?"

"The first world is Eon. It was created to be the capital of the empire, and is home to our greatest industries and institutions. The other three core worlds are Jad, Felis, and Ath. They were the homes of our first warriors, Ston, Alqin, and Eshar. Ston and Alqin were brothers, and Eshar was Alqin's mate. They were the first to bond successfully with the helian symbionts. They created the Eon Empire."

"Wow, that's amazing history."

"Our planets have temperate climates. Eon and Jad are mountainous, filled with lakes of all colors. Felis and Ath are more verdant, with jungles and forests."

Eve smiled. She'd joined the Corps to explore, to see new worlds. "They sound amazing."

"I'd like to show them to you one day. I think you'd like them, Eve Traynor."

They looked at each other for a long moment, and she felt the connection between them like a tangible thing. Her chest tightened.

Suddenly, the ground started vibrating. A chime sounded on Davion's wrist.

Eve looked toward the setting sun.

"Biome change," Davion said grimly.

Eve straightened. "Well, bring it on. I'm hoping for a pretty beach, gentle waves, and some palm trees."

CHAPTER EIGHT

"Snow. Really?" Eve threw an arm up in the air. "Have I told you how much I hate this planet?"

Davion listened to Eve with a smile, the ground still shaking through the biome change.

Snow started drifting down all around them, and beneath them, the ground heaved. Davion pulled her back until she was pressed to his front.

In front of them, they watched mountains spear up into the sky. Eve gasped, her hands gripping his arms. Her fingers brushed near his symbiont and he felt it pulse.

He frowned. Strange that it responded to her.

Eve gasped again and he looked up. Sand flowed away through cracks in the ground. And more snow continued to fall.

Finally, the shaking stopped.

"Holy hell." Eve arched her head back.

Above, clouds churned over fierce, rugged mountains.

The snow was falling fast and the temperature was dropping.

"Let's go, Earth warrior."

Her nose wrinkled and they set off through the snow. "I really would have preferred a beach."

Despite her complaints, she trekked tirelessly. The terrain grew rugged, and it wasn't long before they were sinking knee-deep in snow.

"A sadist designed this place," she muttered.

"It wasn't intended for pleasure or fun."

"No shit. How much farther to the rest station?"

"An hour, unless the snow gets worse." He looked at the sky. "There's a storm coming in."

The clouds churned, getting darker and darker. The trees around them were all a deep, dark green, with some red foliage.

As they continued on, Davion felt a skitter across his senses. Nothing moved in the snow-covered surroundings, but he couldn't shake the feeling that they were being watched.

Eve sensed it as well. He saw the way she looked around, her shoulders tense. They moved in closer together. Somewhere in the distance, a creature let out a long howl.

Her steps slowed.

"What?" he asked quietly.

"I'm not sure." She scanned around. "You sense it, right?"

"Yes. But I can't see or hear anything. Only a feeling." Davion reached out again with his enhanced senses. There was no sign of anything. "We have to keep moving."

They passed through a line of trees, and Eve stopped again.

"There." She pointed.

Davion spotted strange marks in the snow. They moved closer. The markings were small and there were a lot of them.

"Footprints?" She frowned, as she crouched beside them.

"No creature that I know of." He circled around the markings. "But Hunter7 can generate some unique wildlife."

Thwap.

Thwap.

Something enclosed around Davion, squeezing him, and he was whipped up into the air.

Cren. A net had closed around him, his arms trapped at his sides. And the net was still squeezing tighter.

He turned his head as far as he could. The net was made of some sticky, black, web-like substance. He was hovering well above the ground.

"Davion!"

He managed to look down. Eve had avoided her net, which was hanging empty beside his. She had her blaster in hand.

"Hang on," she said.

The net squeezed tighter, digging into his skin. He gritted his teeth, pain spiking through him.

He watched Eve climb a neighboring tree. She grabbed the lower branches, pulled herself up lithely, then started to climb. When she came level with him, her intense gaze landed on him.

"Two shakes and I'll have you free." Her muscles bunched, and she launched herself at him.

She hit the net, sending it swinging. She clung on, her face not far from his.

Then, over her shoulder, he spotted lights bobbing through the trees. He frowned. Someone was headed in their direction.

There was no other sentient life on Hunter7. It created beasts, but not other warriors. That meant only one thing.

Cren. He heaved in a breath. "Eve, the Kantos are coming." This was their trap.

Her head swiveled, her jaw tightened. The stubborn line of it was getting pretty familiar. "I'm getting you down."

"There's no time. This is a Kantos trap. It'll be hard to free me."

"I don't care." She pulled out the knife she'd claimed at the healing station.

He heaved out a breath. "They're getting close." He moved his hand enough to touch hers where it gripped the black rope. "I'm ordering you to go."

Her blue eyes flashed. "I don't follow your orders, and I'm *not* leaving you." She started sawing at the net.

"Then we'll both be prisoners."

She cursed, looking conflicted. He saw her blade was having no effect on the tough, web-like substance. "Leaving is the easy option. I don't abandon anyone. *Ever.*"

He heard the Kantos now—that incessant clicking they made.

He didn't want Eve in the Kantos' hands.

His heart thudded against his chest. "Eve, they're almost here. You won't have enough time to free me. This black substance is near impenetrable. Go. I don't want both of us to get caught."

Her curse was ripe.

He touched her hand again. "Go. Now."

She looked like she was going to argue. "Damn you, Davion."

Now, she used his name. She shot him a heated glare, then let go of the net. He turned a little, fighting against the gripping pain of the netting, and watched her hit the snow in a crouch.

She looked up at him for a long second. He could see the lights had almost reached them.

Then Eve turned and ran, disappearing into the trees.

Davion sagged, releasing the breath he'd been holding. He knew she'd hide her tracks and make it difficult for them to track her.

She was safe.

He wouldn't have to watch them torture her, and mar that fascinating skin, mark the stubborn jaw.

The Kantos soldiers stepped into view, gliding on their four legs, and clicking to each other.

A large one looked up at him. An elite. The Kantos leaders looked like the other soldiers, but were taller, their hard, brown skin a little paler in color.

War Commander. The guttural-sounding words echoed in Davion's head.

The Kantos elite couldn't speak aloud, except for the clicking they used to communicate with the others of their kind. But they could communicate telepathically.

Davion glared at the newcomers.

SITTING CROUCHED at the top of a tree, Eve watched the Kantos circle Davion. They lowered his net to the ground.

Bastards.

She leaped down. She'd counted seven Kantos soldiers, one of which was an elite, and one bug. This bug looked like a spider, with a sturdy black body, round back end, and six large, hairy legs. It had a row of yellow eyes and fangs. No doubt vicious and hard to fight.

Plan. She needed a plan. There were way too many soldiers for her to take on alone.

She heard a masculine grunt echo through the trees and her hands curled into fists. They were hurting him.

Eve knew they'd torture Davion. They clearly wanted to capture him alive, so they were after something only he could give them. They'd be ruthless in their quest to get it from him.

She gritted her teeth. *No.* They weren't torturing him on her watch.

She snuck closer to the clearing, formulating plans in her head, and just as quickly discarding them. Damn, it was getting darker and darker. Soon, it would be night.

Something rustled in the undergrowth behind her. She whirled. *Had a Kantos circled around and found her?*

A set of glowing, aqua-blue eyes peered unblinkingly at her from the shadows under a tree.

A primal, scary instinct rolled through her, telling her to run. She couldn't see the beast, but it was big.

"Um, hey there." She quickly opened her backpack. A low growl filled the air.

That rumble echoed through Eve, the thing of nightmares.

Great. Could things possibly get any worse? She grabbed a nutrition bar and tore it open. "Here you go, boy."

The food landed in the snow, not far from the creature's hiding place.

Another growl, then a giant, black, wolf-like creature slunk out of the shadows.

Holy shit.

It was big. Its back would come up to her breastbone. It took another step forward, sniffed the food, then gobbled it in one gulp. Then it lifted its fierce blue-green eyes to her.

Without a word, Eve tossed another bar.

The beast inhaled that, as well. It studied her again, a pink tongue lolling out of its monstrous jaws.

"Ah, nice doggie."

All of a sudden, it rushed her. *Oh, God.* There was no time to react. She stared at the creature's huge fangs. It could eat her head in a single bite, if it wanted.

It leaped, hit her, and knocked her back into the

snow. One giant paw rested on her chest. It weighed a ton and Eve wheezed, fighting for air.

Then, a large, wet tongue licked her face.

"Oh, eww."

She looked past the solid, shaggy body, and saw that it was wagging its tail.

"Hey, boy." She gave it a gentle shove. "I can't breathe."

It sat beside her and she sat up.

"You still hungry, huh?"

Eve hoped to hell it didn't want to eat tasty human meat. She opened her pack again and offered the animal some larger nutrition packs.

Unsurprisingly, the wolf devoured them.

Eve had always wanted a pet. It had never been possible because there wasn't enough money for luxuries. Then as an adult, Eve was always gone too much. Hard to have a pet when you lived on a starship most of the time.

The wolf creature finished its meal, then gave her face another lick. Eve grimaced, but stayed still.

Then, the sounds of fighting caught her ear. She tensed, and her new friend did as well. He growled.

Eve rose, eyeing her friend. "You like to hunt, Shaggy?"

Those aqua eyes swiveled to her, shining with intelligence. For a split second, she was sure the animal smiled at her.

"Come on." She hefted her blaster. She wasn't letting the fucking Kantos torture Davion.

With the wolf at her side, she battled through the

snow, creeping closer. They shimmied in under the heavy boughs of a tree, sliding on their bellies. She peered through the needle-like foliage.

Her gut tightened. Davion was battling two soldiers, hand-to-hand. His armor was gone, his helian covered in a familiar black ooze. They were making him fight unarmed, and his chest was bare, exposed to the elements.

Cowardly pricks.

One Kantos soldier kicked Davion hard and he staggered back. Now, she could see the sharp, stinger-like spikes sticking out of his chest and shoulders. Fire licked along her nerves. The Kantos had tortured him, sticking those damn spikes into him.

"Ready, Shaggy? We're going to save my friend and kill some bugs."

Her wolf friend stiffened, his glowing eyes on the Kantos.

She smiled darkly. "Go."

Eve and Shaggy burst out of the trees. She fired her blaster, aiming at the closest soldier.

She'd caught them by surprise. After several laser blasts to the face, the first soldier fell, bright-green blood splattering on the snow. Shaggy let out a vicious howl, rushing at more soldiers. He moved incredibly fast, leaped into the air, and knocked down three Kantos and the bug.

She heard the soldiers shriek, and then the crunch of bones.

Grinning madly, Eve spun. Another soldier was rushing at her, sword raised. "Come on, bug boy."

She fired in rapid succession. Eve ducked and spun, thrusting with her knife. A stronger fighter, this alien jerk blocked and matched her moves. But Eve let her anger coalesce—at her imprisonment, the threat to her sisters and her planet, the damn situation she'd been forced into, and this killer planet.

Eve lunged, her knife cutting in beneath the soldier's arm. She sliced into his hard skin, hearing him grunt. Green blood sprayed.

She turned, lifted the blaster, and fired. The Kantos sagged. When she turned, she spotted one soldier staggering away from Shaggy. The bug was dead, torn to pieces, and the wolf still had two soldiers pinned, their arms flailing. She watched the animal tear an arm off and winced.

Effective, but eww.

She turned, saw Davion was fighting his two soldiers. Not having a weapon didn't slow him down much.

The wounded soldier that had escaped Shaggy headed toward Eve.

She whirled, spinning her knife. Then she charged. The soldier was too slow. She drove her blade up and sideways. It slashed his neck and he made a gurgling sound.

"Not so much fun now, is it?" She stepped back.

There were only Davion's two left.

With a brutal hit, Davion drove one soldier down into the snow, gripped his head, then snapped his neck with a vicious twist of his powerful hands.

Make that one.

The final Kantos looked at Davion, then Eve.

Deciding she was smaller, he turned and rushed at her. He swung his arms above his head.

Eve fired her weapon. He jolted, but kept coming. *Dammit.* She blocked the Kantos' swing with her arm. But the hit was hard, rattling her bones. Pressing her lips together, she shoved against him, driving the Kantos back. He rushed at her again, arm swinging wildly. Grimly, Eve danced backward.

Then her boot hit a rock hidden under the snow and she fell.

Shit.

She landed on her side and rolled. She looked up, just as the Kantos drove his sharp arm down. It hit the snow beside her head. Just inches away.

"Eve!" Davion powered toward her, his face coldly enraged. She felt the wave of his fury wash over her.

Another swing of the Kantos' arm, and Eve rolled to the other side. The hard edge of the alien's arm clanged on a rock.

Then a long, low howl broke through the clearing.

Shaggy bounded toward her, sending snow spraying in his wake.

Scowling, Eve rolled again, pushing to her feet. Did she look like a damsel in need of rescue?

She spun, swinging her knife. At the same time, Shaggy sailed through the air, his jaws closing over the head of the Kantos soldier.

Eve scowled. "He was mine, Shaggy."

The animal paused for a second, eyeing her, before he closed his jaws. Bones crunched.

Hands on her hips, Eve turned. Davion stopped beside her.

His gaze skated over her body, then he eyed Shaggy. He shook his head, but he was smiling. "I see you made a friend."

Shaggy was now happily eating the Kantos soldier. *Ugh.* "One with dubious manners."

"Hunter7's creatures are not designed to befriend anyone." Davion tilted his head. "Actually, it's unheard of."

She lowered her knife. "I'm a friendly woman."

His smile widened. "I know."

"And I just rescued your fine ass."

He shot her a look.

She pointed the knife at him. "You owe me, War Commander." She pulled the antidote injector off her belt and held it up. When he held out his wrist, she dripped the fluid onto the black ooze trapping his symbiont.

"I want samples of that when we get off this planet," he said.

"If you ask nicely."

She saw the blade of her knife was chipped. It had clearly been designed for medical use, not fighting. She strode over toward the other downed Kantos. It was unlikely they'd have any weapons—Kantos used their bodies as weapons—but it was worth taking a look.

"Eve, watch out!"

Davion's shout had her automatically leaping back… just as a Kantos spider bug leaped out of its hiding place in the trees.

Eve felt a brief flash of pain as the creature swiped at her with one of its clawed legs.

Incensed, she threw her knife at the creature's eyes. The blade hit, and the creature let out a shriek.

But Shaggy was on the move again. The wolf jumped onto the Kantos bug, taking it down with a vicious growl. The bug flailed.

"Dammit." Eve straightened. "Everyone's stealing my action today."

"Eve."

Davion moved close, his eyes wide. His hand clenched on her bicep.

"It's all good, except my new friend hogs the action."

But Davion didn't smile. "Eve."

His tone made her frown and look down. Bright blood splattered the snow on the ground at her feet.

What the hell?

Then she looked at her chest and the diagonal slash across her suit.

Blood was soaking into her suit. That's when the pain hit her, like a line of fire across the chest.

Dizziness swamped her, her vision blurring. She pitched forward, but she didn't hit the snow. Instead, strong arms caught her.

CHAPTER NINE

Davion lifted Eve into his arms. Blood. There was so much rich, red blood everywhere.

"Eve."

She looked up at him, blinking slowly. "Warrior." Then she smiled at him. "You're so pretty." She ran her fingers along his jaw. "Stinking gorgeous."

By Alquin's axe, she was hurt bad. And he had nothing to stop the bleeding.

The huge wolf-like creature trotted over. It looked at Eve and whined.

Davion looked at his wrist. He'd managed to grab his gear that the Kantos had stripped off him. He needed to get her to the rest station and heal her. Then, she'd need time to recuperate.

He checked the map, his gaze settling on the closest rest station. Then he broke into a run, shouldering through the trees and ignoring the falling snow. The wolf loped beside him.

Davion pushed down the pain of the spikes still embedded in his chest. Every step made them burn, but Eve needed help. He could tend his own wounds later.

"Fucking Kantos," she muttered.

"Hold on, Eve. They'll pay. For everything." For every drop of blood of hers they'd spilled.

"Hell, yeah." Her head lolled against his arm. A grimace crossed her face. "Hurts."

"I know, *shara*. Hold on."

"Hate...Kantos."

"I won't let them destroy your planet, Eve."

She smiled goofily at him again. "There's a nice guy under the war commander."

"Not really." He was known as focused and ruthless. It seemed she brought the good out in him, along with this fierce need to protect her.

The creature beside him suddenly cut in front of Davion and roared. Davion stopped, pulling Eve closer. A white, humanoid-looking beast covered in white fur was lurking beneath the trees in front of them. The thing had claws as long as knife blades.

Cren. Davion froze.

But the creature that Eve had nicknamed Shaggy leaped forward. It snarled and growled. The white-furred beast snarled back.

Then they charged at each other. In a frenzy of growls, the two animals fought.

"Help him," Eve murmured.

Davion looked at her pain-filled blue eyes. No warrior had ever helped a creature on Hunter7...and yet, he was beginning to realize he couldn't deny this woman what she wanted.

Shifting Eve in his arms, Davion lifted his arm up and commanded his symbiont. The scales on his arm morphed, and three sharp, spinning blades shot out from his wrist. They whistled through the air, over Shaggy's head, and cut into his opponent's shoulders.

Blood spurted and the white beast screamed.

"I love that symbiont," Eve mumbled. "I want one."

Davion didn't tell her that some warriors didn't survive the bonding with the helian. It was a dangerous, arduous transition.

The bleeding creature staggered off into the trees, Shaggy growling after it. But Davion let out a sharp whistle, and the wolf turned, trotting back to his side. Hitching Eve higher, Davion continued on, Shaggy moving close to his legs.

The snowstorm was imminent. The wind was howling, stirring up the snow around them in large eddies. Cold was seeping into Davion's veins, making each step painful.

He hadn't gone much farther when Eve lost consciousness.

"Eve! Eve!" Panic rose in Davion's throat. He wasn't used to feeling this sense of concern and helplessness.

Shaggy whined.

But his enhanced senses brought him the sound of her heartbeat. She was alive. That calmed Davion…a little.

"She's alive, Shaggy. But we need to heal her."

Lowering his shoulder, he pushed against the wind.

The darkness closed and it was hard to see where they were going. The snow thickened and the temperature dropped even more. In his arms, Eve shivered.

Cren. They were lost in this snowstorm and he couldn't see a thing.

Then Shaggy yipped.

Davion turned...and spotted a light in the trees.

He pushed through some low branches, and then he saw the structure. It was a dome-like shelter made entirely of ice. But the inside glowed with warm light.

Davion fought through the knee-deep snow and finally reached the door. He shoved it open and a wave of warmth hit him.

Shaggy brushed past him and he let the animal in before slamming the door closed behind them. In the small entry, Shaggy glanced through the inner doorway that led to the main rest station space. He let out a huff, then flopped down in front of the door. Davion wasn't fooled. The animal was keeping guard.

That was enough for Davion.

He moved inside. The large, round room was covered by the arched dome above. Through the clear dome, he saw the snow falling outside, dancing in the wind. Any other time, if things weren't so dire, he'd appreciate the view.

He made his way to a pile of furs and supplies in the center of the space. On the far side of the dome, he spied a set of stairs leading down to some subterranean room. But he'd worry about exploring later.

He laid Eve on the furs, the pain in his chest making him swallow a grunt. For a second, his gaze snagged on her blood-covered chest, his heart lodging in his throat. He turned to the supplies, pressing his palm to the box to open it.

Davion pulled out the medical supplies. He formed a blade with his symbiont and then cut Eve's suit off. It was ruined.

He wasn't sure about what drugs to use with her different physiology, but since Terrans and Eon were similar enough, he decided to risk it.

He pressed a healing stim into her neck and injected her. Her face was so pale and she'd lost so much blood. All to rescue him.

Eon warriors were bred and trained to understand that they might sacrifice their life for the empire. To think of this small, fierce woman risking her life to save him...

He pushed her tangled hair off her face. The words she'd spoken to him earlier rang in his head. *Leaving is the easy option. I don't abandon anyone. Ever.*

Eve was used to people leaving or letting her down. Her father, unintentionally. Her mother. The Space Corps.

Pushing the unfamiliar, churning emotions aside, Davion began to clean the ugly slash wound across her chest. It wasn't long before he decided her color looked better. The stim was working.

He reached into the supplies and pulled out a small vial. It glowed bright red and he knew it was infused with a small amount of bio-organisms similar to his helian called havv. The havv had been created by the warrior Eschar. He squeezed some of the thick, red fluid onto Eve's cut, and he watched as it moved, seeping into the wound. The red glow intensified as it set to work, and her skin began to knit together.

Davion blew out a breath of relief. She was safe. In a few hours, she'd be healed.

As his gaze ran over her, the fear seeped out, and was replaced by something else.

He couldn't help but look at her body. Her breasts were larger than an Eon female's and topped with pretty, pink nipples. He took in her flat belly, toned legs, and the tiny strip of her black panties.

He blew out a breath. *She's healing, you Cren-cursed idiot.*

Davion grabbed the edge of a blanket and flicked it over her. Then, the knowledge that she was taken care of was like flicking a switch on his own pain.

His chest throbbed, bolts of agony shooting through him. Sucking in a breath, he looked down at his chest. He still had several of the Kantos' spikes sticking out of him. They needed to come out, or his symbiont would get his body to heal around them. Each one was also tipped with poison to enhance the pain, and he could feel it making him sluggish.

First, he needed some food, because he was running on fumes. And he knew removing the spikes himself was going to hurt. A lot.

Davion ate some nutrition bars, carefully watching over Eve. She slept deeply, a side effect of the healing the havv was stimulating.

Then he pulled out some medical tools, gripping some large tweezers in one hand. He pinched the end of the first spike.

He pulled.

The pain was intense, tearing through him. Gritting his teeth, he worked the spike loose, knowing the poison was causing most of the burning pain. The barb jerked free.

Davion sucked in air, his vision blurring. He was drenched in sweat, and his chin dropped to his chest.

As dizziness washed over him, he decided to just sit and rest for a moment.

EVE DREAMED of Kantos shrieks and burning pain. But when her eyes opened, there was no pain. In fact, she felt good.

She cautiously assessed her body and realized she was lying under a thin blanket. She was warm and cozy. She looked up, seeing a clear, ice roof and the snowy night beyond.

When she raised her hand to her chest, she felt nothing but smooth skin. She was healed.

She pulled the blanket around her and sat up.

"Take it easy."

Suddenly, Davion was there, helping her sit. He was also holding a hot drink. Sudden and immediate hunger and thirst swamped her, and her stomach rumbled. She took the drink, gulping it down as quickly as she could, despite the temperature. *Mmm.* It was warm and sweet.

When she lowered the glass, Davion was sitting beside her. While she felt great, he looked like death warmed over.

She frowned. He was still smeared with blood. Her jaw tightened. She was all healed, and the idiot still had several Kantos spikes sticking out of him.

Her stomach growled.

He smiled at her, although it looked strained. "That's a side effect of the havv." He held out another cup. "Some soup."

She took it, sipping the broth. Flavor burst in her mouth. Oh, God, it was good. "Havv?"

"The healing organism I used on your wound. It's related to the helian."

"Well, I can't argue with the results. I feel great."

"I also gave you a healing stim."

She nodded. "Thank you." Her gaze dropped to the spikes. "Did you use one on yourself?'

"No."

Men. She rolled her eyes.

A faint smile tipped his lips. "Can't. Not until the spikes are out, or my body will heal around them."

She nodded. "Well, we need to get those out."

"I managed to get a couple out, but it was a...painful process."

Eve eyed the two, bloody spikes resting beside him. She read between the lines—it had been agony and he'd only managed the two.

She set her soup down and wrapped the blanket more securely around her, tucking one end between her breasts. She moved closer to him. Up close, she could see the lines of pain bracketing his mouth.

She nodded, grim determination flowing through her. "Then let's get them out, warrior."

Reaching for the heavy-duty tweezers sitting beside him, she moved to face him. She got a grip on the first spike.

"Ready?"

"Do it."

She tugged. Slowly, the spike slid out. Davion groaned and she looked up. His jaw was clenched.

"Keep…going," he gasped.

Steeling herself, Eve dropped the first spike and got a grip on the next one. She pulled. Air whistled through his teeth.

"Got it." She dumped the bloody spike with the others. Nausea welled. His face looked ragged. "You can do this, Davion. We're almost there."

He managed a tight nod.

The job felt never ending and Eve felt his pain, even though he tried to hide it. Finally, she tossed the last spike onto the ground.

"Are you okay?" She smoothed a hand up his arm.

A stiff nod. "My helian is helping to heal me."

She blew out a breath. "Good. Do you need some of that havv stuff?"

"No."

She didn't want to stop touching him, but forced herself to lift her hand. She might have this insane attraction to Davion, but she couldn't let herself get attached. She couldn't risk feeling too much. Looking for a distraction, she picked up her cup of soup.

"You could have died, Eve."

She sensed something else radiating off him now. "But I didn't. Thanks to you."

"I told you to run." His gaze settled on her, hot and accusing.

She sipped her soup. "Yep."

"Didn't you hear me?"

"I heard you."

"Then you misunderstood my words."

"No."

He sucked in a breath.

"I wasn't leaving you to be tortured and killed, Dav."

At the shortening of his name, his eyebrows rose. "That is not my name."

"It suits you. I like it."

"Infuriating woman."

She smiled. "You're such a charmer."

He tilted his head. "Are all Terran women like you?"

"No, I'm one-of-a-kind. I tend to piss off or intimidate most Terran males as well."

"I am not surprised." He glanced at her chest. "I need to check your wound."

He said it matter-of-factly. Eve tried to be the same as she set her empty cup aside. She lay back on the mound of furs and loosened the blanket.

When his big hand flicked the blanket off her, leaving her chest bare, she swallowed. When his fingers brushed the skin between her breasts, she pulled in a breath. She looked down, watching his darker, bigger hand move over her skin. She liked this man's hands on her.

He quickly checked where she'd been slashed. It was now perfectly healed.

"I am very glad the Kantos didn't kill you," he murmured.

"Me too."

A sudden tiredness fell over her and she struggled to keep her eyes open. Panicked, she grabbed his arm. "Davion—"

"Don't worry, Eve. This is another side effect of the healing. Sleep. I'm here. I'll keep watch."

She sagged and felt him lift her up, moving her back to the center of the furs. He tucked the warm blanket securely around her.

"Promise?" she murmured.

His hands moved to her hair, playing with the strands. "I promise. I won't leave you."

"No one's ever watched out for me before." She sighed. "And everyone always leaves me." Sleep pulled her under.

But there was a part of Eve that was aware of his big body sliding in beside hers. She turned her head to his chest and held on. His arms closed around her, holding her tight. And Eve moved deeper into sleep, feeling safer than she ever had in her entire life.

When she woke the next time, she stared up. And blinked.

Holy cow. She was alone in the furs, and the snowstorm had cleared.

It was still night time, but now she was staring up into beautiful blue-green lights dancing in the dark sky above. *Wow.*

She sat up, deciding she needed to wash. She spotted a clean shirt set out beside the furs and smiled. It was a warrior-sized shirt. It would be like a dress on her.

She pulled the shirt on and glanced across the room. She spotted a shaggy, black tail near the front entry. She crept closer and inside the entryway, she saw Shaggy was asleep at the door. She reached over to pet him and he pushed lazily against her palms before settling back to sleep.

Where was Davion? Eve looked around and saw the stairs.

She headed down. She saw light reflecting off water, the shimmer dancing on the dark walls of the subterranean room.

There was a pool of water in one corner. She moved closer and stuck her fingers in it. It was crisp and cold, not warm at all. She shivered.

Still, she really wanted to be clean. And there was still no sign of Davion. She pulled her shirt off, and quickly washed until her skin was covered in goose bumps. She pulled the shirt back on. God, it was so nice to be clean.

Turning, she spotted a doorway. There seemed to be a second room down here. As she walked toward it, she heard muffled sounds.

As she got closer, she realized it was the rhythmic sound of fists hitting something.

She paused in the doorway, leaning against the carved-out frame. Of course, the Eon would put a gym in their rest stations. Heaven forbid if a warrior actually rested.

Davion was pounding a huge bag suspended from the rocky ceiling. He was pummeling it with powerful, angry hits and kicks. He was shirtless, the muscles in his back flexing. His skin gleamed with sweat, and she lost herself in watching him.

Desire was a steady thrum in her body.

He must have sensed her, because he turned.

Molten eyes were on her and she felt seared to her bones.

CHAPTER TEN

Eve stood there, something burning through her. Her insides shivered, heat rising.

Davion turned, and she let her gaze travel over his powerful body. He wore no armor now, just man and muscle. Just Davion. His chest was bare, and only a simple pair of black, loose-fitting pants sat low on his hips.

She saw the faint marks on his chest from his injuries. And man, the pants draped over those muscular legs and perfectly toned ass.

He stalked toward her.

Her pulse spiked. "Dav—"

"You're healed?" His voice was deeper, harsher.

"Yes." Her pulse pounded.

"Take your clothes off."

Heat and shocking desire arrowed through her. He was so close that she could smell his scent, feel the heat of him.

She never took her gaze off his eyes. The air around them throbbed. His words were an order, but she also knew he was waiting for her to make a choice.

WOULD IT HURT? To have him just once?

Eve slid her hands beneath her borrowed shirt and hooked her fingers in the sides of her panties. She pushed them down and they fell to her ankles.

Davion made a raw sound, and then he was pressed against her. His hands gripped her shirt and shoved it up.

They both moved, and his arms wound around her, lifting her off her feet. She wrapped her legs around his waist and he carried her a few steps. She felt a cool wall behind her back.

His mouth crashed onto hers, his tongue pushing between her lips. With a moan, she kissed him back, her hands sliding into his thick hair.

Eve's body seemed to detonate. They kissed wildly, tongues delving deep, his fingers biting into her ass. His cock—hard and very insistent—pressed against her belly. She wanted to touch every hard inch of him, explore that unbelievable body. But what was burning between them right now was too hot and fierce for either of them to have any patience.

Davion hitched her higher and she felt his hand working between them, pushing his trousers out of the way. Then she felt the thick head of his cock nudge her folds.

Air caught in her chest. Her fingers clenched on his shoulders.

He surged inside her. Her sharp cry echoed off the walls. He was big, filling her and making her stretch.

"Eve." A guttural sound.

She moved her hips against him. "Move."

He started thrusting inside her.

Yes. It was hard, rough, and raw. She felt taken, possessed, wanted.

He grunted with each thrust, and she tugged on his hair. The sensations ripping through her were so intense she could barely breathe. Suddenly, he swung her away from the wall. He strode across the room, setting her on a carved-stone bench.

Eve lay back, watching her big, gorgeous war commander above her.

Davion kept thrusting, driving deep. He pushed one of her legs up, giving him better access to her. His deep grunts echoed in her belly and his gaze burned through her.

Then, she watched as his gaze traveled down her body, down to where they were joined. A look crossed his face and it made her belly spasm. Oh God, she couldn't handle this overwhelming rush of pleasure.

He ran one hand down the path that his gaze had taken. Oh, that look on his face...

Eve had never felt so desired.

Then his hand slipped down and found her clit. She guessed Eon and Terran women weren't too different. She bucked against him and a wicked smile edged his lips. He stroked the small nub, rolling it between his big fingers.

"Davion!"

He growled, his thrusts increasing. "Say it again."

"Davion."

"Again. And this time come for me."

"Davion." His next hard thrust triggered her orgasm. It hit Eve like a supernova. She arched off the bench and felt him lean over her, thrusting harder.

The power of his thrusts shifted the bench several inches across the floor. Then he lodged deep inside her, threw his head back, and roared through his own release.

EVERY MUSCLE in Davion's body felt loose and relaxed. He was still lodged in Eve, feeling her tight body ripple around his cock.

He pulled in a shuddering breath. The pleasure filling him was like nothing he'd experienced before.

He looked down, and large, blue eyes looked back at him. He was very pleased to see they looked slightly dazed.

Stroking a hand up her torso, he marveled again at this woman. With her fascinating strength and undeniably female body.

"Wow," she said, voice husky.

His gaze went back to her face. The need to possess stormed through him. He wanted her again. He'd just had her, but he wanted to discover everything about her.

He wanted more.

She licked her lips. "Uh, it is sort of a little late, but I'm guessing you're healthy. Sexually."

"My helian ensures that."

"Good. And I'm the same." Her nose wrinkled. "I have been in prison for months." She licked her lips. "So, this is pretty crazy, but we, uh, survived some extreme circumstances, so I guess…"

His cock was still inside her and she was trying to be rational. He pressed his hands to the stone bench on either side of her. That shifted his hips forward, pushing his still-hard cock deeper into her.

She moaned.

"Go on," he said.

"…well, adrenaline and extreme circumstances. We saved each other's lives. Sex is an understandable conclusion."

His little Earth warrior trying to stay sensible and distant. Trying to control everything. He thrust inside her again and her lips parted.

Mostly, he knew she was protecting that battered heart of hers that she kept locked up.

"This isn't about any of that," he said.

Her eyes widened. "It…isn't?"

"No. Now, I'm going to spend the rest of the night fucking you. Finding out every way you like being pleasured."

"I…" She licked her lips. "I'm definitely okay with that."

Davion drank her in. The flushed face, the swollen lips, the sexy, full breasts. His time with her had told him that she let very few people close.

He wanted in.

He wanted Eve.

And he was beginning to realize that his need

wouldn't be assuaged in just one night. It had nothing to do with burning off adrenaline.

No, Davion wanted much more. And he was a man who was used to going after what he wanted. He was also a good war commander, and excellent with battle strategy. If he told his Eve what he was thinking, his little Terran would panic.

He skimmed his hands under her, pulled his cock out of her, and lifted her off the table. Then he strode into the other room.

By the pool, he set her down and then reached for one of the cloths stacked beside it. He dipped the cloth into the water and knelt in front of her.

He cleaned her skin, checking her chest and noting that she was completely healed. He circled her breasts, watching her nipples pebble. He dipped the cloth in the water again, then he slid it down her flat belly and between her thighs. He took his time cleaning her.

Her hands slid into his hair. He'd noticed she liked his hair.

"Davion—"

"Shh."

She fell quiet and let him tend to her. When he was done, he scooped her back into his arms and carried her up the stairs.

"I've been carried by you more than I ever have in my life," she said.

Good. He liked knowing that.

He laid her back in the furs. He'd spent a lot of time imagining fucking her here—bare skin on fur, his mouth on her as the sky arched above them. He stretched out beside her. She was looking up at the lights dancing above.

"So beautiful," she said.

He looked at her. "The most beautiful thing I've seen."

Her gaze met his, her cheeks going pink. "I'm not beautiful, Davion."

"Beauty means different things to different people, Eve. And it is more than one thing." He stroked her hair. "I love this hair. As black as the darkest depths of space."

"I got it from my grandmother. She was Japanese, and they tend to have black, straight hair."

His hand moved lower, cupping her breasts. "And these are very pretty."

She rolled her eyes. "Typical man."

It was more than just her looks. She was his tough warrior. He'd watched her fight and defend, kill and protect. But he liked that for all her toughness, she still blushed when he looked at her.

Davion shifted down, pressing a kiss to where the claws had sliced her. He kept kissing, moving to one nipple, sucking it into his mouth. He loved the noises she made and when he blew softly on her nipple, he liked watching her writhe in the furs.

He could spend all night on those breasts, but he kissed his way down her stomach, and slowly nudged her thighs apart. She had a tiny strip of dark hair above her sex, and the rest of her was pretty and pink. He needed to taste her.

Lowering his head, he put his mouth on her, licking and sucking.

"Oh, God, yes." She wrapped one thigh around his head, pumping up to his mouth.

He worked her, loving her musky taste. The sounds she made drove him crazy.

He kept lapping, reading each husky cry and move of her body to see what she liked best. Soon, she splintered apart, coming hard and screaming his name.

Need pounded inside Davion, his cock so hard it was painful. He moved to cover her, but she reared up, surprising him. He let her push him onto his back on to the furs.

Eve climbed on, straddling him.

"My turn, warrior."

Desire twisted in his gut. She rose above him. So gorgeous.

One of her hands circled his cock and she pumped it, once, twice. He groaned. Then she rose up on her knees, notched his cock between her legs, and sank down.

Their groans mingled. Davion watched her take him inside her.

She moaned. "So big."

"So tight."

She started to move, sensations barreling through him —hot and electric.

She watched him, a sexy smile playing across her face. "Get ready for a ride, War Commander."

He gripped her hips. "I can take whatever you give, Sub-Captain."

As she rode him, taking him deep, Davion knew without a doubt that he'd spoken the truth.

CHAPTER ELEVEN

Davion woke with a female sprawled all over him.
    He tensed. He rarely slept the night with his bed partners. Then he remembered, his muscles relaxing. *Eve.*

Her face was pressed to his chest, her hands holding him, and one slim leg tossed over his thigh. He also had an arm around her, holding her close.

He felt a fierce rush of contentment. It wasn't an emotion he was used to. Satisfaction, success, fulfillment, yes. Contentment was something new. He pulled her closer, stroking her back, his gaze on her face. She looked relaxed, and he realized that he'd never seen her without the determined edge her features always held.

No surprise, but he felt need stir. He wanted her again. All of her.

He'd spent the night taking her until they'd both collapsed in exhaustion. He had a few still-healing scratches on his back and ass from her nails.

But it was more than just wanting more of the intense pleasure. Davion wanted to see all of her—happy, sad, angry, content.

He'd made a shocking, startling realization.

Eve Traynor was *his*. His woman, his partner. The one person he knew had been born for him.

Davion had never claimed anything solely as his. He'd lived for his job and his people. His parents had dedicated their lives to the Eon Empire and had instilled the same loyalty and sense of service in Davion.

He knew there would be many people in the Eon leadership that would frown on him claiming a woman, let alone a Terran woman. But he didn't care.

Breathing in her scent, he looked up through the ice dome and saw that the morning had arrived. A clear, blue sky arched overhead.

He sighed. Unfortunately, in order to have any chance of survival, they had to get moving.

Davion was well aware that the path ahead wouldn't be easy. And he wasn't just talking about the journey to the comm station.

Him telling Eon High Command that he'd claimed a Terran female would cause some chaos. And then there was the Kantos' brazen attack on him, and the imminent invasion of Earth to deal with.

Davion's jaw hardened. He was done ignoring the Kantos. It was time to end their voracious greed.

Eve stirred, her eyelids flickering open. She froze for a second, then looked at him and smiled.

Yes, Davion could spend a lifetime waking up to that smile.

Her hands spread over his skin and she pressed her lips to the center of his chest. She peppered him with small kisses and slowly moved lower.

"Good morning," he murmured.

She made a humming noise. "Morning."

Davion lay back, allowing himself to enjoy the strong, sexy woman who was unafraid to take what she wanted. Unafraid to tell and show him what she liked.

Eve shifted, her dark hair spilling across his gut. She gripped his cock and he pulled in a breath. Then she licked him.

Cren. He bucked. She sucked his cock between her lips.

Her mouth was wet and warm, and she took her time —teasing and taunting. She kept the suction hard, and he had to fight to keep from shooting down her throat like an untried warrior.

Enough. He knifed up and spun Eve flat onto her back. Then he was on top of her.

"I wasn't quite done, War Commander."

"Yes, you were."

He slid his aching cock into her slowly. Her moan was long and loud.

"Faster." She dug her nails into his ass.

"No."

They'd attacked each other plenty of times through the night, driven by their fierce attraction. This time, he wanted to show Eve something else.

With unhurried movements, he pushed her arms above her head. Her lips parted, her eyes fluttered closed.

"Keep them open, Eve."

She did, her gaze fastening on his. He drowned in blue.

"*By Eschar*, you're gorgeous."

Her cheeks flushed. Had no one ever told her that before?

She tried to get him to move faster, but he kept it slow and steady, but firm. He felt her shift restlessly beneath him, her cries increasing. Her body clamped down on him.

"You're squeezing my cock so hard," he groaned.

"Davion!"

She arched her back and broke. She panted through her orgasm. *Cren*, he loved watching her come.

Her release had his own roaring closer. He increased the speed of his thrusts now. Her legs wrapped tightly around him and he hammered into her.

"Give it to me," she cried. "I love the feel of you inside me."

His orgasm hit hard. He thrust deep, groaning through the blinding release. When he collapsed, he rolled, pulling her close to him.

"Well, War Commander, I always knew you had skills and talents..."

He slapped her ass and she laughed. He loved the sound.

But unfortunately, reality was a harsh mistress. "We have to—"

"I guess we should—"

They both spoke at once.

Eve smiled, pushing her tangled hair from her face. "We need to go."

He nodded.

She rose, and again his cock twitched. That long, naked body never failed to arouse him. He watched as she grabbed some fresh clothes from the rest-station stash. Then she sauntered toward the stairs.

"I'm going to freshen up."

While she was gone, Davion dressed, and found some food. He set some out for her and munched on several packets. Next, he opened the weapons locker and selected some things he knew Eve would like.

When Eve returned, she was wearing Eon Warrior black. The clothes weren't quite as formfitting as her space suit, but seeing her in the attire made for a warrior made him smile.

Suddenly, Shaggy bounded over, nuzzling Eve. With a laugh, she patted the wolf and gave him some food.

"Is my big boy hungry? I'm very glad you were watching the door and not getting an eyeful of the show." She held out some more food. "Here you go."

Shaking his head, Davion started packing supplies into one of the backpacks.

"Right." Eve's nose wrinkled. "Off we go for an unpleasant, cold walk in the snow."

Davion helped her slide a backpack on. "The biome will change soon. Besides, if you get cold, my Earth warrior, I'll keep you warm."

She rose up on her toes and kissed him. "Why thank you, kind war commander."

"I have something else for you." He held up a simple, Eon-forged sword. It was strong, well-balanced, and sharp.

Her lips tipped up and she took the weapon. She swung it through the air. "It's perfect."

"I thought it would suit you."

She looked at his face. "A lot of Eon things appear to suit me."

He wanted to kiss her again, but he knew if he did, he wouldn't stop. He watched her sheath the sword and then he urged her toward the door.

With one last glance at the rest station, they headed out, Shaggy bounding ahead of them.

EVE HIKED UP THE HILL, her boots kicking up snow.

Davion had draped some sort of fur coat over her, so at least she wasn't cold. She glanced at him and just looking at her war commander gave her a warm glow.

Her war commander.

God. The night replayed through her head. It had been the best night of her life. The best sex of her life. The best orgasms she'd ever had.

He was the best man she'd ever met. A man who met her move for move, who matched her, understood her. Respected her.

He was also a generous lover who'd worshiped her.

Eve blew out a breath.

"You okay?" His hand gripped her shoulder and squeezed.

"Yeah." God, that handsome face.

He nodded, then grabbed a stick and threw it for Shaggy. The animal dashed away to fetch it.

Eve felt something uncomfortable pierce through the warmth in her chest. Davion was a man who was extremely dedicated to his people and his military career. He was Eon, she was Terran.

If they managed to get off this planet alive, where the hell did that leave them?

God, falling for Davion Thann-Eon was a bad idea. Falling for any man was a bad idea.

Their time on Hunter7, their joint fight for survival, had forged a bond between them. But when they returned to reality…

Hell, she'd abducted him. His people hated hers. And there was nothing she could do to change that.

Suddenly, there was a rumble beneath their feet. *Shit*. She looked up and saw Davion scanning their surroundings.

"Biome change?" she asked.

He nodded.

Nearby, the ground began to part, creating a giant chasm. The shaking rocked her back, the land rising up beneath her feet.

With a cracking sound, another chasm split the ground, this time, right between Eve and Davion.

"Eve!"

Hell. She ran, leaping across the widening gap, throwing her arms forward.

The edge got closer but she realized the gap was too wide. She wasn't going to make it.

Davion leaned out and grabbed her hands. She slammed into his arms.

She rested against his chest for a second. Beside them

trees fell, swallowed whole by the ground. Dark rocks, like wicked teeth, rose up.

Jeez, what was next?

Davion held her close, shielding her. The snow melted away, and she felt the heat rising off the ground around them. Shaggy let out a howl.

And then, lava bubbled up from the chasm. *Oh, great.*

The ground stopped shaking and she straightened. "My God."

Ahead of them lay a vast lake of lava. All around, black, twisted rocks rose up, and small rivers of lava oozed sluggishly toward the lake. No trees or vegetation remained.

Then a thought hit her. She spun. "Shaggy!"

They both looked around. There was no sign of the animal.

A surprising pang hit her. "He's gone." Just like that. "Does he even…exist anymore?"

"I don't know," Davion answered.

Her heart felt heavy. "I hate this planet."

Davion frowned, scanning the horizon. Then he pointed. "There's the comm station."

He pointed to some jagged mountains that speared up on the other side of the lava lake. A metallic glow gleamed on one ragged spike of rock. Below it was a straight cliff face.

Eve sighed. "Well, unless you can fly, it looks like we'll have to climb."

"I'm not fond of climbing."

She raised a brow. "Don't tell me there is something the fearsome War Commander Thann-Eon isn't good at."

"I can climb, I just don't enjoy it."

"Of course, you can do it." The man could clearly do anything.

"Come on, my Earth woman."

They started trekking around the edge of the lava lake. Golden-red, molten rock bubbled in places and in the center of the lake, sprayed up like a geyser. She and Davion had to leap across several small lava streams that flowed into the lake.

Out of curiosity, Eve crouched, scooped up some rocks, and tossed them into the lava. She watched them sizzle. *Real, burn-your-skin-off lava.*

They were getting close to the rocky spear that held the comm station when she heard a noise behind them.

She spun, lifting her weapon.

Nothing.

"Davion?"

"I sense a heartbeat. Wildlife."

Eve didn't spot any ugly-ass creatures, ready to eat them. She turned and started walking again. She heard a hiss.

She spun again. This time, she saw a scaled tail flicking back and forth from behind a large rock.

Wonderful. They were about to meet some new, toothy, dangerous resident.

Davion was tense, watching and waiting.

The reptile burst out from behind the rock. It moved fast, on all four legs, its sturdy body covered in dark, oily scales. It looked like a giant lizard. Its jaws were filled with needlelike teeth.

Shit. It charged straight at Eve, leaping into the air. She raised her weapon.

Then she saw bright aqua eyes and a lolling tongue.

"Wait!" She lowered her sword.

"Eve!"

The reptile hit her and took her down to the rocky ground.

And licked her face.

The heavy weight of it crushed her chest and she couldn't breathe. The reptile's body wriggled.

"Shaggy?" she wheezed.

There were more excited wiggles and another lick.

"Shaggy!" Ecstatic, Eve sat up, pushing his lizard-like body off her.

Davion helped her to her feet.

"It's Shaggy!" She grinned. "But he's changed to suit the biome."

"Yes."

"Well, he's not so shaggy anymore." She patted him. "But you're still you, aren't you, boy?"

The lizard made a coughing grunt.

Eve looked at Davion. He was watching her with an intense look on his face.

"Davion?"

He ran a hand over her head. "I'm glad your friend is still with us."

"Me too."

"Now, come. Let's get to the comm station."

CHAPTER TWELVE

Davion leaped up the sleek, black rock face, caught a handhold, and heaved himself upward. His symbiont had made his gloves and suit sticky to help him climb.

Beside him, Eve was climbing like a Felis tree-jumper. The small animals were the best climbers on the planet. She was also smiling.

"This is not fun," he bit out.

Her smile widened as she climbed past him. "I love climbing."

They were high above the ground. A fall would have them shattering bones on the jagged rocks below. Not fun at all. Shaggy was also climbing up the cliff face with ease, body pressed flat, and seemingly defying gravity.

Davion looked up. The comm station was on the peak above them. Not far to go.

Eve kept climbing, and he took a second to admire her moves. Then he noticed something just above her head. The black rock was glowing orange. Like it was getting hot.

"Eve, look out!"

She froze, lifting her head.

Suddenly, the orange rock burst outward. Eve started and lost her grip. She fell.

Heart pumping, Davion reached out one arm. He snagged Eve's hand, breaking her fall. His other hand gripped hard to the rock, and for a second, they hung there. Eve's eyes were wide as she looked up at him.

"I've got you." He heaved her up, pulling her close to him.

They clung to the cliff face and together, they watched the orange-gold lava pour out like a waterfall to the ground below.

"Wow." Eve's voice was a little shaky. "If I wasn't completely freaked out right now, I'd think that was beautiful."

Davion pulled in a deep breath. Not much rattled his Eve. He looked at her face. Yes, he loved looking at her, and he loved that sleek body of hers, but he also loved her resilience and toughness. His woman just didn't give up.

And more than anything, he wanted her off this deadly hunter planet.

She reached around and gave his ass a pat. "Okay, get moving, warrior."

Then she reached up and started climbing again.

Davion shook his head and followed. Fearless.

Soon, they pulled themselves over the edge of the top. *Thank the warriors.*

As they crouched on the flat platform, the comm

station gleamed welcomingly in front of them. It was a small, dome-like structure, and it shimmered a faint blue from the energy shield protecting it. It was made of clear, hexagonal shaped tiles.

"Why's this one got a shield?" she asked.

"Some do, depending on the biome. My guess is that it's to protect it from any lava flows."

Davion rose and walked toward it. He found the entrance to the dome and pressed his palm to the nearby panel. It chimed. He stepped inside, Eve right behind him.

In the center of the dome was the comm unit. A cover slid back, and he pressed his hand to the controls. His symbiont shifted, a thin cable extending from the armor at his wrist and plugging into the comm unit. He quickly created a message to send to the *Desteron*.

"How long will it take them to come?" Eve asked.

"I'm not sure. They had maneuvers planned—"

Boom.

They both threw their hands out, grasping anything within reach for balance. They looked up. A projectile hit a rock nearby, throwing shards and chunks of stone in all directions, with many pinging against the energy shield.

"Fuck," Eve said.

They sprinted for the exit. They ducked out of the station, drawing their weapons. Shaggy crouched nearby, hissing.

Davion turned and saw two large Kantos flying creatures in the air. Their giant, leathery wings flapped up and down as they hovered in place.

"Great," Eve muttered.

Both creatures were saddled with riders, and armed with missile launchers on either side of their solid bodies. As they watched, one of the missile launchers turned bright red and then fired.

Davion spun. "Watch out—"

Boom.

The projectile hit the comm station. Davion was tossed into the air, and out of the corner of his eye, he saw Eve hurled away from him. They both landed hard on the rock, rolling close to the edge of the cliff.

Cren. Davion gripped onto the rock to stop his slide. "Eve!"

She was closer to the edge, her upper body hanging over it. She looked dazed, a thin trickle of blood dripping down her temple. She shook her head.

"Eve, move slowly..."

She turned her head, and when she realized her precarious position, she quickly scrambled back.

Davion reached her, yanking her up beside him. "We'll be safer in the comm station."

She nodded and they sprinted back toward the station. Another missile whizzed overhead, and they ducked. Davion whistled for Shaggy.

The three of them dived into the comm station just as another missile hit the shield. The comm station shook.

Eve grabbed the central unit to stay on her feet. "You sure the shield will hold?"

"Yes, but it won't hold out indefinitely against prolonged missile fire." They had to get out of there.

And the only way down was an arduous, dangerous climb...with flying Kantos shooting at them.

Then, Davion saw something else fire from the second flying creature. A dark cable whizzed out, wrapping around the comm station. Another matching cable fired from the first Kantos creature.

"What the hell?" Eve said.

Davion frowned. He didn't like this.

Suddenly, the entire comm station lurched. The two creatures flapped their wings, flying higher and higher. The station lurched again, and Eve bumped into Davion. He wrapped his arm around her. Shaggy skidded across the floor.

One more violent jolt and the entire comm station broke free of its foundation.

Eve gripped his arm. "Holy fuck."

Shaggy let out a wild round of guttural growls.

The comm station sailed out over the edge of the cliff, suspended between the two Kantos creatures.

Eve and Davion stumbled, then both braced themselves on the central unit, knees bent. The comm station bobbed and swayed as they soared through the air.

"I have a really bad feeling about this," Eve said.

Davion suspected that was an understatement.

"I HATE THIS PLANET." Eve kept her feet spread in a vain attempt to keep her balance.

"I don't think you can blame Hunter7 for this one, *shara*," Davion said.

She wondered what *shara* meant, but now wasn't the time to ask. The station dome jerked wildly, and they both jolted again, falling to their knees.

"Well, I fucking hate the Kantos too."

"I'm right there with you," he said darkly.

"We need a plan, warrior. We need to get off this thing."

Shaggy was sitting on his butt, looking through the shield and growling at the flying creatures outside. Eve glanced down and her stomach rolled. The dark, rocky ground, crisscrossed with rivers of lava, lay far, *far* below them.

The Kantos were taking them somewhere, and she could only guess it wasn't anywhere nice. Plus, the farther away they were from the comm station location, the less likely Davion's people could find them when they arrived.

Then a thought occurred to her. "Did your message get sent?"

A muscle ticked in his jaw. "I'm not sure."

Great. So they had no idea if help was coming, and even if it did, the *Desteron* rescue team would arrive to find nothing more than the remnants of what was once a comm station.

Davion looked at her. "Ideas?"

"How strong is the shield, if the Kantos aren't pounding it with missiles?"

A crease appeared on his brow. "Strong."

"Then we need to cut the ropes free."

Davion stilled. "What?"

Before he could process her idea, Eve pulled out a

knife, and quickly moved over to the exit. She pushed her way through.

"Eve!"

Outside, the wind whipped at her hair. She turned, pressing her palms to the dome and started climbing. She used the small, raised joints between the hexagonal tiles as handholds. As the station bobbed, she fought to keep her grip.

She made her way toward the closest rope. It arched through the air, up toward the giant flying Kantos. The damn creature made her think of a dragon.

One of her boots slipped on the slick shell of the dome. She slid a few inches down. *Shit*. She pressed hard to the dome, gripping on.

"Eve, this is too dangerous."

She turned her head and saw Davion making his way up to her.

"We need to get back to the ground, Davion. Or they are going to drop us in a camp full of Kantos, and we're as good as dead anyway."

She scrambled closer to the rope, then pressed her knife to it and started sawing. The cable was sinewy, fibrous, and gross.

Davion's big body brushed hers. "Even if the comm station shielding stays intact, the plummet could kill us."

"The Kantos will kill us anyway. I prefer to do it on my own terms."

She heard his grunt and she kept sawing the blade. In moments, she was halfway through the cable, and she smiled grimly.

Suddenly, the rope jerked wildly, and Eve almost

tumbled off the edge of the dome. She glanced up, and saw the Kantos rider staring at them. He'd spotted what they were up to and was flying erratically, trying to stop them.

Eve starting cutting again.

Davion raised his arm, a blaster forming on his arm. He fired a bolt of blue energy at the Kantos.

The flying Kantos gave another wild dip, and this time Eve slid down the dome, her knife flying out of her hand.

"Eve!"

Davion grabbed at her, but missed.

She shot over the edge of the dome and out into the air.

Oh, God. Her heart lodged in her throat and she frantically windmilled her arms. Skydiving with no parachute was definitely a bad idea.

Something blue snapped around her waist. Suddenly, she jerked upright, and was no longer falling.

She dangled in the air below the dome, a blue rope circling her waist. She gripped it and the realization clicked. A symbiont rope. She looked up.

Davion was pressed against the dome, his arm extended toward her, and the blue, scaled rope linking her to him.

Eve felt a pulse along the line. It was alive and powerful.

Davion started pulling her in. As soon as she got close, he reached out and yanked her into his arms.

"*Cren.*" He buried his face in her hair.

"Nice save, warrior." She burrowed her face into his neck, waiting for her pulse to stop racing.

"No more falling."

"I'll do my best." She noticed he'd left the blue rope around her waist.

The comm station bobbled, bringing her back to the situation at hand.

"We still need to cut the ropes." She'd lost her knife in her fall, but she wasn't giving up.

Without stopping to think, Eve touched the blue rope, running her hand over it. The blue flowed over her hand and a knife formed on her wrist.

Holy cow, that was so cool. She had no idea that Davion could share his symbiont with her. She crept closer to the Kantos cable and moved her hand. The blade sliced right through it.

The dome wobbled in the air and began to fall.

Davion cursed, pressing her against the dome so that she was pinned to it by his big body.

"Back inside. Now."

She nodded, and together, they shimmied downward and slid back inside the station.

Inside, Shaggy was sliding around the room, clearly unhappy and agitated. The dome had begun to swing wildly, and Eve realized that one Kantos flying creature alone wasn't strong enough to keep the dome in the air.

She saw the lone creature flapping its wings like crazy, but they were continuing their downward trajectory.

Fast.

Hell. She watched the rocky ground rushing up at them.

"Warrior…oh, shit."

Davion yanked her down and covered her body with his.

Suddenly, the black of his armor started shifting and moving. Her lips parted, and she reached up to touch it. It flowed over her, binding them together in a protective cocoon. She gasped and she saw Davion frown.

Then they hit the ground.

There was an ear-splitting crash, and a jolt that made her teeth rattle. They were tossed around, the dome rolling like a ball. Eve held on to Davion for dear life.

CHAPTER THIRTEEN

Davion commanded his helian to retract, and pushed to his feet inside the dented and smashed comm station. The armor flowed off Eve and back into his own.

When he saw her blinking up at him, he released a breath.

But shock still coursed through him.

Not from the attack, or the fall from the sky. Eve had commanded his symbiont, and it had responded. Then it had acted to protect her.

His helian had connected with her.

He'd never, ever heard of a partner or mate that could control an Eon warrior's symbiont. It was unheard of.

"Hey, are you okay?" Eve cupped his cheek, her eyes concerned.

He nodded. There would be time to ponder the incident later. "Let's find some cover."

"Yeah."

Shaggy scampered over, running circles around them. The animal had clearly survived the fall without harm.

A shadow moved over them and Davion looked up. The remaining flying Kantos was circling overhead.

"Come on."

They turned and had taken two steps when he paused. He sensed...something. Something big.

"What?" she asked.

There was movement up on the ridge nearby. Davion straightened.

Rows of large, six-legged Kantos bugs crested the ridge. They were all saddled and topped with soldier riders.

"Ah, hell," Eve muttered.

"Run." Davion jerked her in the opposite direction.

They both sprinted, Shaggy running beside them. They leaped over several meandering streams of lava.

Behind them, Davion heard the thunder of the Kantos bugs giving chase. He turned his head and saw them streaming down the ridge.

"They're coming!" he shouted.

A buzzing hum filled the air. Shaggy growled and hissed.

The glow of lava appeared ahead and Davion cursed. This river was wider. Too wide to jump. They cut left, running along it.

"Shit, Davion. Look."

Directly in front of them was an enormous lake of lava.

They were trapped between the Kantos and the lava. *No.*

Eve stopped, her chest heaving. "Nowhere to go."

No.

She gripped his arm. "We fight, warrior."

Davion wrapped an arm around her and yanked her close. He kissed her—hungry and desperate. "We fight."

His sword formed, elongating on his arm. But Eve had no weapon.

Then he held out his arm to her. She stroked his sword, then touched the scales of his armor.

His symbiont shifted. A small part of his armor flowed across to her arm, circling her wrist. A smaller sword formed on her arm.

She lifted it, staring at it in wonder. "I had no idea you could do this."

"I'm not doing anything, you are. I've never heard of it happening before."

Her mouth dropped open. "What?"

But they were out of time for explanations. Davion turned. The first wave of Kantos were getting closer.

Eve stepped up beside him. Then she winked at him.

Fearless. They both nodded, then ran toward the incoming bugs. Shaggy bounded past them, eager to attack.

"Bring it!" she shouted.

They hit the lead wave of Kantos, dodging out of the way of thundering legs. Davion sliced out with his sword, cutting through armored arms and legs. He leaped up, spinning, and cutting a rider out of his saddle.

Nearby, he saw Eve swinging her sword. Blue energy drifted off it like smoke. She slid in low, knocking over several soldiers, before she jumped, cutting them down.

Still running, she leaped onto a rock, took two steps, then jumped. She landed in the center of several bugs and attacked with a vengeance.

Amazing. *His.*

The leg of a bug smacked into Davion, sending him stumbling. He dived, somersaulted across the rocky ground—narrowly avoiding a pool of lava—and came up swinging.

He slashed through several more bugs. Adrenaline pumped through him, the heat of battle settling on him, fueling him. He saw Eve land on top of one of the bugs, yanking the rider off.

She sat in the saddle and the bug bucked beneath her. She flew off and Davion jumped, catching her midair. They both landed in a crouch.

"Thanks." She smiled briefly at him, and he saw the battle heat reflected in her eyes.

She spun and sprinted back into the mêlée. He watched as she swiveled, kicking one Kantos soldier in the chest.

"How do you like that, bug boy?" She swung her deadly sword, shouting as she fought. "Second wave!"

Davion saw them coming. He raised his weapon, the blue glowing brightly.

The bugs hit them like a wave. He fought his way closer to Eve, and soon they were back to back, fighting in perfect unison. He swung in low, while Eve slashed high, swinging to cover him. Nearby, Shaggy fought with his usual enthusiasm, tearing into the Kantos.

But soon, he felt his muscles start to ache. Sweat dripped into his eyes and he knew they were tiring. Eve was still fighting, but her swings were a fraction slower. He turned his head, that incessant clicking of the Kantos driving him crazy. More bugs were marching toward them. That was always the Kantos advantage—numbers. They liked to swarm and overwhelm.

Soon, Davion and Eve were surrounded. There were far too many Kantos for them to fight off all of them. He watched Eve cut down another bug.

He wanted Eve to live. His chest tightened. He'd trade anything to keep her breathing and unharmed.

"Eve—"

She read his tone. She spun, her clothes splattered with green Kantos blood. Her hair waved around her face in the breeze. "We fight, Davion. We *never* give up."

He dragged in a breath. There was that grim determination that he knew came from her very soul. He nodded.

They kept fighting, and soon Davion was drenched with perspiration. His arms burned, and Kantos claws had opened up a wound on his back. He was moving slower and slower. Even Shaggy was flagging.

But the swarm of bugs wasn't getting any smaller.

He was a master of strategy. He achieved success by calculating odds and outcomes, and now, his chest tightened. The Kantos were waiting for them to tire.

Suddenly, the ground started to vibrate beneath them. Nearby, several cracks opened up in the ground. Lava poured down through it.

"Biome change?" Eve yelled.

A large crack opened up beside him and Eve leaped over it, landing beside him.

Davion frowned. It felt different. "I don't know."

The rumbling increased, and he saw several of the Kantos stumble. The ground heaved, more cracks forming.

One of the Kantos bugs let out a horrible screeching sound.

Eve lifted her sword. "Come on. You can't be afraid of a little shaking."

More bugs screeched, skittering backward.

Eve laughed. "Cowards."

Davion watched the bugs pull back. *By Ston's sword.* What was happening?

"Come on, you ugly bugs." Eve stepped forward. "Fight!"

Davion sensed movement behind them and turned to look over his shoulder.

His gut clenched.

"Eve." He grabbed her arm.

She turned and her face froze.

Behind them, a giant lava creature was rearing up out of the lake.

AW, hell.

The Kantos switched their attack from Eve and Davion, to evading the lava creature. The beast was huge, with giant horns and huge powerful arms. It looked like some devil rising out of a horror movie. Shaggy let out a hissing whine.

Lava dripped off the monster, landing nearby in sizzling puddles. Eve and Davion leaped back. They continued to retreat, but they were still trapped between the lava creature and the rows of Kantos fighters.

"Lava beast or Kantos?" she said.

His unique eyes met hers, the blue strands gleaming.

She nodded. "Kantos."

They turned and ran. She let out a whistle for Shaggy to follow. As they sprinted toward the nearest bugs, she saw that many of the Kantos were retreating as well.

Suddenly, the lava creature let out a terrifying roar, and thumped one of its giant fists onto the rocky ground. A huge ball of lava flew through the air. It smacked into a bug, lifting it off its legs. The Kantos' clicking turned into a high-pitched frenzy that hurt Eve's ears.

She kept running, leaping over some rocks. Davion kept pace beside her with ease. Her lungs were working hard and he wasn't even breathing heavily.

God, he was all strength and stamina. She liked him so damn much.

"That way." He pointed through a crack in the Kantos troops.

They changed directions, running through the field of large, scattered rocks.

"Think we're almost out of range of the lava creature," he said.

But suddenly, Davion jerked to a stop and Eve slammed into the back of him.

"Dav—" She looked up. "Fuck."

Ahead, a fresh wave of Kantos soldiers marched toward them, their sharpened arms pointed at Eve and Davion. Shaggy hissed, standing beside Eve, body quivering.

War Commander Thann-Eon. The raspy words echoed in Eve's head.

A tall Kantos elite stepped forward, his four legs moving smoothly. He had the same powerful body with brown scales that the soldiers had, but was a little taller and held himself straighter.

Davion pushed Eve back behind him and she rolled her eyes.

Come with us. The Kantos leader tilted his head, his four yellow eyes gleaming. *Avoid more bloodshed.*

Davion stayed silent, but she felt the tension pumping off him.

"Tell him to go fuck himself, Dav."

More silence.

Frowning, she looked up at him. His face was set, hard.

"You made a grave mistake attacking me," Davion said. "The Eon Empire will not forgive this transgression."

The Kantos leader didn't move. *The time has come for the Kantos to rule the galaxy.*

Davion lowered his voice. "You really think you can beat the Eon warriors?"

With the military secrets we gain from you, yes.

Oh, shit. This was bad. Really bad. Eve swallowed, trying to find a way out.

The Kantos leader tilted his head again. *We can make a deal.*

A deal? Eve blinked. What kind of deal? "Davion?"

The Terran is not important to us.

Davion nodded. "I come with you, and you let her go. Unharmed."

Eve felt like he'd punched her in the gut.

The Kantos nodded.

"No!" Eve shook her head, slapping a hand at Davion's chest. "You are out of your ever-loving mind."

"Eve—"

"No!" The word exploded out of her. "You *know* me. God, I think you know me better than anyone in the damn galaxy. You know I don't want this."

Something flickered in his eyes. "You matter to me." His words stole her breath away. His voice lowered so the Kantos couldn't hear. "They'll hurt you to get to me."

"No, they won't, because we'll fight." She grabbed his hands.

He stroked her wrist. "You stay safe. You stay alive. Wait for my men to arrive."

"No." Panic slid into her veins. He was leaving her.

Davion stepped away from her.

"If she's harmed, our deal is off," Davion said darkly.

The Kantos leader nodded. *Armor off, War Commander*.

Eve was horrified when Davion's armor retracted. The Kantos soldiers swarmed him, hitting and kicking. Shaggy moved forward and Eve grabbed him.

A different type of soldier flowed forward on four legs. He had a stockier body than the other soldiers and gray, hard skin. He dripped black ooze on Davion's symbiont, and then he lifted one arm and stabbed it against Davion's side. She felt a flare of energy in the air.

Davion's body shuddered. The Kantos was delivering some sort of electric shock.

No way. Eve exploded into action, kicking at the closest soldier.

The rasping mental voice of the Kantos leader echoed in her head. *Do not harm her.*

They didn't attack her, but they blocked her path to Davion.

"Eve." He was still standing, his hands curled into fists and his jaw clenched. She heard the pain in his voice.

She saw two soldiers kick Davion's legs out from under him. Tremors still wracked his body. The gray Kantos shocked him again.

Fury ripping her open, she spun, fighting the soldiers. Shaggy leaped up beside her, growling.

The Kantos leader waved a hand, turning away.

Two soldiers started dragging Davion.

An elbow rammed into Eve's chest, knocking her back. Shaggy growled, jumping in to protect her. Another soldier thrust with his arm, trying to get Shaggy to back off.

But Shaggy wasn't giving up. He flew at the Kantos' head. A second soldier lunged in, thrusting his sharp arm into Shaggy's body. It pierced the animal right through.

"No!" Eve screamed.

They shoved Shaggy away and his body flew into Eve. She fell to the ground, the animal a dead weight on top of her. Eve struggled to try and get him off her.

She felt the blood. It was warm as it trickled over her.

"No. No." She looked into Shaggy's face.

He made a horrible sound, clearly in terrible pain.

"It's okay, boy." She pressed closer, managing to drag herself out from under his weight. She put pressure on the wound, but the way he was bleeding told her the Kantos had hit something vital. The red blood gushed through her fingers.

She looked over and saw the Kantos were mounting up on their bugs. They'd dragged Davion onto one bug and he was heavily bound. His head hung limply.

Before she could move or plan, the leader raised an arm. The Kantos turned their bugs and took off.

Emotions swelled inside Eve's chest, making it hard for her to breathe. She watched, helpless, as Davion was taken away from her.

She swept her arm across her forehead, brushing the sweat from her brow. She stroked Shaggy's side, listening to his labored breathing. She felt like she'd been cut open. Like she was bleeding, just like Shaggy.

Murmuring to the animal, she kept stroking him. "I'm here, boy." His breathing started to falter, and a rock settled into her throat.

She waited with him, stroking and talking gently until his lungs stopped, and his chest no longer rose and fell.

He let out his last, shuddering breath, his eyes closing. Closing her own eyes, Eve pressed her face to his scaly hide.

She was all alone. Davion was gone—a captive of the Kantos. He'd be tortured and killed. And Shaggy was...

She pulled in a shaky breath. Tears threatened and Eve hated the fact. She *hated* crying. Even as a little girl who'd lost her father to death and her mother to alcohol, she'd lain dry-eyed in bed. She hadn't wanted to be weak.

Instead, she embraced the anger boiling deep in her gut. It exploded and she surged up, pissed and furious.

She found a dead Kantos soldier nearby and kicked the body. "Assholes!"

Kantos. Fucking Kantos. They destroyed everything good.

She stumbled over to where Davion's things had been dropped. She found his wrist screen. It was cracked, but when she touched it, the screen flickered to life. It showed a map of the area.

She slipped it onto her wrist, watching as it shrunk down to adjust to her smaller size.

A map indicating the nearest weapons cache appeared on the screen.

Perfect.

On the other wrist, she still had some of the black scales from Davion's symbiont. She stroked them and felt a pulse. It made her feel less alone.

Then the screen chimed and her chest hitched. The ground started to change.

Biome change.

She stood there, watching as the lava started to drain away. The mountains shrank, like they'd deflated. A wave of golden grass sprang up, crossing the black rock like a wave. It kept growing, brushing her boots, then her waist, then her chest.

And Eve found herself standing in an endless grassland.

There was nothing around her, but in the back of her

head, she wondered what beasties the long grass was hiding.

She set her shoulders back. It didn't matter. She had a job to do.

Damn you, Davion. She was pissed at him, as well. Sacrificing himself for her. He'd made her fall in love with him.

Love. Jeez, the one thing Eve had vowed to avoid had hit her when she'd least expected it. Fear and excitement mixed inside her. Well, she sure as hell was going to rescue her man and then give him a piece of her mind.

Eve started to jog in the direction of the cache, pushing through grass. It wasn't too far away, but she wanted to get organized. She'd wait for nightfall, then track down Davion and rescue her man.

A screeching noise pierced the air and she swiveled. An abandoned bug burst out of the grass, its saddle empty. Its six legs skittered, its two giant compound eyes staring at Eve. It had a streak of green blood on its side, but looked otherwise uninjured.

Eve's gaze narrowed on the alien creature. *Slight change of plan.* She strode toward it.

CHAPTER FOURTEEN

When Eve approached the metallic weapons cache nestled in a tiny clearing in the grass, she worried about how she was going to open the damn thing. But as she got closer, the symbiont scales resting gently around her wrist slid over to cover her hand. When she pressed her palm to the panel, it chimed, and the metallic dome opened.

Inside, lay a small supply of food, drinks, and basic medical supplies.

She quickly tore into the nutrition packets, then gulped down some water. Next, she found an injector and pressed a stim to her neck, wincing at the sting.

Straight away, energy seeped through her tired, battered body. She grabbed several injectors and slid them into her pockets. Davion might need them.

Right, time for weapons.

She sorted through a strongbox filled with different Eon weapons. She picked carefully, finding several Eon blasters that she'd always lusted over. At the same time, she tucked a few knives into her belt. There were even some grenade-type devices, and she smiled as she helped herself to a few.

Finally standing, she slung a blaster over her shoulder. She was ready. She pulled in a deep breath.

When she headed back to her bug, it skittered nervously, trampling the grass. It had taken her a while to get the damn thing to obey her, but they'd come to a cautious truce. Luckily, these bugs were clearly bred to be compliant transportation.

"Too bad, bug head. I have a man to rescue."

As she climbed into the saddle, the alien let out an unhappy squawk.

Eve didn't give a fuck. She urged it on, and they were soon moving fast through the grass. It made a swishing sound.

She quickly adjusted to the bug's odd gait, and she leaned forward as they moved swiftly toward the last place she'd seen Davion. They passed through a patch of grass that had huge, globe-shaped purple flowers on top. Eve eyed the flowers warily but they passed without incident.

At the spot on the map, they circled around a few times. It didn't look anything like it had when the Kantos had taken Davion. *Damn.* There was no trail or tracks to pick up.

But then the bug tensed, like it sensed something. It took off in one direction and she gave the creature the lead.

Hope you know where you're going, bug. They raced

through the grass and ahead, she saw the large orb of the orange sun sinking toward the horizon. Night would be here soon.

They continued on and soon, the shadows grew. Eve wondered how she was going to see in the dark, but as twilight fell, she noticed light coming off the grass.

The grass glowed a faint gold. *Cool.*

Then a familiar clicking echoed through the night and the bug slowed. In the distance, she saw a large gleam of light. *Gotcha.*

Smiling grimly, she urged the bug on. Not too far from the Kantos camp, she slipped off the bug and tied its reins to a clump of grass. "You stay here. I'll be back."

Then Eve moved forward, quickly and stealthily, using the grass for cover. Above the sweep of grass, she spotted the heads of several saddled but rider-less Kantos bugs. They weren't moving, so she guessed they were secured.

A long, pained masculine groan came to her on the wind. It was coming from just beyond the bugs. Her heart clenched. They were torturing Davion.

Dropping to her belly, she slithered through the grass and up a gentle hill. Reaching the top, she paused, parting the grass and peering down.

On the other side of the slope was a large clearing of trampled grass. Davion was trussed up between some posts set in the ground, his arms held out to the sides. His bare chest was covered in wounds and cuts, and too much blood. His symbiont had been confined, so he couldn't use it.

Bile rose in her throat. *The bastards.*

It looked like they'd finished their torture for now. Davion's chin was resting on his chest, his hair covering his face. A group of Kantos soldiers were walking away from him.

She swallowed the lump in her throat. "Hold on, warrior."

As one, the Kantos soldiers moved toward several long lines of other soldiers. She watched as they assembled themselves in rows, standing still, their arms by their sides. It looked as though someone had pressed their off buttons. They were clearly resting, just standing there, still and unmoving. It was creepy.

Eve waited a few more minutes. She didn't see any of the Kantos move, or even twitch.

Now or never. Moving quietly, she pushed through the grass, her gaze locked on Davion.

At the edge of the clearing, she looked around, checking for sentries or anyone left to guard Davion. None of the Kantos moved. She raced across the clearing to Davion. As if it anticipated her needs, her symbiont moved, creating a knife on her wrist. She reached up and started cutting his ropes.

Before long, they broke, and he fell. She caught him, but he was dead weight, and drove her down to her knees.

He groaned.

"Hey, warrior," she said softly. "I need you to help me."

His beautiful black eyes threaded with blue opened. They were drenched in pain.

"You... Dream?"

"Nope."

He blinked rapidly, eyes slowly clearing. "Eve?"

"The one and only. You really didn't expect me to leave you, did you?"

"So stubborn."

From her pocket, Eve pulled a pressure injector. She touched it to his neck and dispensed the stim. Then, she pulled out the antidote and freed his symbiont. Her hands slid up his body, and she gently touched the wounds on his chest. She couldn't treat them yet, but as his dark armor flowed up his body, covering his chest, she figured it would help stop the bleeding for now.

"Up," she urged.

With her arms around him, and him helping as much as he could, she got him on his feet. It wasn't pretty or graceful, but he was up. He was still weak and he was heavy as hell. They stumbled across the ground, heading to the edge of the Kantos camp. Eve kept a careful watch, certain they'd be mobbed by soldiers at any second.

But the Kantos stayed, unmoving, in their creepy little group.

Eve released a breath. This was too easy and that made her nervous.

They moved into the long grass. She shouldered through it as they crept uneventfully through the faint glow from the vegetation. Finally, they reached her bug.

Davion eyed it. "You're joking."

"Nope, this is our ride."

She helped him onto the beast, and she heard him try to stifle his groan of pain. Then she climbed on behind him.

She nudged the bug and got it moving. She tilted her wrist to look at his screen and quickly spotted a rest station. Her priority was getting him healed.

"Eve—"

"You can get angry with me for rescuing you later."

He turned his head. "I wanted you safe." He released a breath. "But thanks."

Warmth moved through her. "You're welcome, warrior." She leaned forward and pressed her lips to his.

DAVION WAS IN AGONY. He had internal injuries, but he was hiding it as much as he could from Eve.

She rode like a woman possessed, pushing the bug they were riding as hard as she could. Soon, he saw a brighter blue light glow through the grass ahead. The rest station.

Blinking back the fatigue and pain, he gripped the bug hard to stop from falling off. Then a thought occurred to him. "Where's Shaggy?"

The jagged silence behind him made his gut tighten.

Eve stopped the bug and slid off. "The Kantos killed him." Her voice was flat.

Cren. Davion awkwardly maneuvered and slid off the bug. When he hit the ground, his knees shook, but he managed to stop himself from collapsing.

He grabbed her and pulled her to his chest. Her forehead rested against him and he just held her. The animal had come to mean something to both of them.

She pulled back. "Come on. We need to get these injuries sorted out."

"The bug—"

"Can it lead the Kantos to us?"

Davion shook his head. "It can track its own kind, but has no special senses to track us."

"Good." Eve slapped the back of the bug and it took off with a shriek. It disappeared into the grass.

She slid one arm around Davion and parted the long grass with the other. Several huge, gray boulders were heaped in a pile, surrounded by grassland. The rest station was nestled in among the rocks—a small dome made of shiny gray rock—and looked far smaller than the one they'd had in the snow biome. He climbed up the rocks, Eve helping him.

They entered the station, closing the door behind them. Lights clicked on and Eve gasped.

The space was like a tiny grotto. The air was warm, greenery grew down the walls, and to one side, was a small flow of water trickling out of the wall like a tiny waterfall, falling into a small, blue pool. On the other side of the dome was a hammock strung up for resting, and containers of supplies.

At that moment, Davion wavered from the pain, swaying on his feet.

Eve gripped him tighter. "Come on, warrior."

She helped him over to a rock ledge, and he collapsed with a grunt. Then she tore through the supplies. She pulled out the glowing, red healing havv. His own symbiont was already working hard to repair the damage to his body, but the added havv would help. She wet a cloth and started cleaning his wounds.

"The havv was created by our first warrior, Eschar." He started talking to take his mind off the pain. "It's the same color as the sacred, symbiont-infused gem that is housed in her temple."

"You worship your first warriors." Eve squeezed the havv on and it moved along the cuts and wounds.

"We don't consider them gods, but we revere them. Remember and honor their service." He sucked in some air. "There was a fourth warrior, Cren. He was disgraced when he tried to kill the others. We remember him for his disloyalty." Pain flared and Davion pressed his lips together.

"Can you have another stim?" she asked.

He nodded and she pressed it to his neck. "Talk to me. Distract me."

"You know my story."

"You didn't tell me exactly why Space Corps threw you in prison."

"Ugh. That is a crapola story." She smoothed a hand over his chest.

He pressed his hand over hers. "You're a brilliant, resilient fighter, Eve. Loyal, reliable, and dedicated. An asset that shouldn't be rotting in a cell."

She smiled at him. "It was because of the Haumea Incident. My ship, the *Orion*, encountered a Kantos ship near Haumea. That's an ellipsoid dwarf planet out beyond Neptune's orbit in our solar system." Her smile faded away. "My captain—"

"The incompetent idiot."

"Right. Bobby J. Hathaway. His mother is a Rear-Admiral in Space Corps."

"Ah." Davion was completely focused on her, forgetting his pain.

"Yes, *ah*. Anyway, the Kantos were attacking a cargo ship en route to a colony on the moon of Triton. Every suggestion I made on how to lure it away and attack it, was rebuffed. Bobby had his own ideas."

When she fell silent, Davion touched her cheek. "And?"

"The cargo ship was destroyed. All fifty-five crew were killed." Her voice was flat. "The *Orion* took fire and we lost three of our best engineers."

"And they forced you to take the fall."

"They needed someone to blame, and Rear-Admiral Hathaway ensured it wasn't her son." A look crossed Eve's face—half sad, half angry.

And Space Corps, the organization Eve had trusted and given her loyalty to, had abandoned her.

A spasm of pain rocketed through him and he groaned. Eve made a sound of sympathy and gently kissed his shoulder, right beside a nasty gash. He just stared at her dark head.

She nodded to the hammock. "Why don't you rest?" She pressed some nutrition packs into his hands. "Eat and sleep." She scowled at him. "Don't think I don't know that you're hurt worse than you're letting on."

He smiled weakly at her. "I'm healing."

"Good." She squeezed his hands. "Because you scared the hell out of me."

"At first light, we hunt for those sons of Cren," he growled.

She smiled. "Oh yeah."

Davion tugged her closer, needing the feel of her. He pressed his lips to hers in a slow, unhurried kiss.

Then she pulled back. "You need rest."

"I need to clean up first." He started stripping off the rest of his gear. Naked, he rose, and Eve hurried to him. He didn't tell her he was already feeling much better and stronger.

She helped him sit down beside the small waterfall. Unlike the other rest station, the water here was pleasantly warm. When he reached to scoop up some water, she stopped him. Dipping a clean cloth into the water, she turned and started running it over his chest and arms.

Moving behind him, she bathed his back, then moved again to kneel in front of him. Davion breathed deep. The cloth made steady strokes over his chest, his abdomen. Eve was staring at his skin, and the look on her face was one he couldn't quite identify.

Each stroke made his pain drift away. Each stroke had desire igniting and flaring inside him.

She shifted between his thighs, the cloth moving down. As she washed his cock, it hardened under her touch.

Her gaze flicked up to his, need meeting need. "You're hurt—"

"Already healing." He waved at the knitting cuts on his skin. "I need something else far more important now."

Eve rose and he lifted his hands, unfastening her clothes.

"You should rest," she said.

He ignored her, yanking at her pants. He stood, pulling her in for a hard, needy kiss.

Together, they stepped into the pool, close to the small waterfall. The water was enjoyable, and Davion took his time cleaning the blood and sweat off her skin. She ducked under the water and emerged, her dark hair plastered to her head.

She nudged him back onto the rock edge and slid onto his lap. He shifted, his cock rubbing against her slick folds. She made a small, husky sound and then she sank down on his cock.

"Oh, God, you fill me up," she moaned.

He gritted his teeth at the pleasure of her tight warmth squeezing him.

Then she started to ride. There was nothing sweet or patient now, it was hard and fast. He pressed his mouth to hers, drinking in her taste and swallowing her cries.

Neither of them lasted long. They hammered out all their frustration and fear on each other until he slammed her down hard, driving his cock deep inside. She cried out, her nails scoring his skin as she came. Then Davion poured himself inside her.

He pressed his cheek to her neck. Yes, he was feeling much, much better.

He rose, Eve in his arms. She made a small sound of protest, but he ignored her. He carried her to the hammock and climbed in with her.

They snuggled in the mesh netting, tangled up with each other. He pulled one of the thin blankets over them.

"Eve—"

"Shh. We're safe right now. Let's just rest."

They settled in the hammock, Eve wrapped around him. He buried his face in her hair and was surprised to find himself quickly sliding into sleep.

When Davion woke, she was still asleep. Looking down at her still form, he felt a huge rush of love. He, one of the most dedicated Eon Warriors, had fallen in love. Completely. With everything he had.

Eve Traynor was his mate. She eased things inside him, made him feel more than he'd ever felt before, and she could command his symbiont.

He stroked a hand down her arm, marveling at the softness of her skin. He cupped one full breast, rolling her nipple between his fingers.

She woke with a moan. Then, he maneuvered her so that she was sitting up, straddling his chest. The hammock rocked in response.

"Something on your mind, War Commander?" she purred.

"Yes." He gripped her hips and jerked her forward. Her knees slid up either side of his head so she was straddling his face. *Perfect*. He put his mouth on her.

"Oh, my God."

Her hands gripped his hair. He licked and sucked her. *By Eschar*, he loved the taste of her.

She slid her hands up her belly and cupped her breasts. His cock pulsed. She was the sexiest, hungriest lover he'd ever had.

Then she scooted backward, moving out of range of his mouth. She curled a hand around his cock.

"No." He grabbed her hand. "I want to watch you come first."

He shifted her hand until it slid between her thighs. Their joined fingers brushed her clit and she jerked. Davion moved a hand over hers, his finger alongside hers, rolling her slick clit. She lifted her hips, panting, and twined their fingers together. She slid them lower, then pushed so both their fingers slid inside her. She let out a husky cry.

Cren. So damn sexy. He worked their fingers inside her, her hips shifting restlessly. Then he shoved her hand away, slid two fingers back inside her, and thumbed her clit.

"Davion…I…yes…"

She threw her head back, the hammock rocking wildly. Her cries echoed off the walls.

Then she dropped forward, her hand sliding down to grip his cock. He groaned and arched up.

"Yes. Now I get to drive you out of your mind." She stroked him, then grabbed one of his hands, and wrapped it around his cock with hers. They pumped him together.

"You are so beautiful," he said.

Her face flushed. He meant every word. He loved that she was so open in her reactions with him, that she trusted him.

"Now, put me inside you," he ordered.

With a smile, she moved again, the hammock swinging. She straddled him, aimed his cock between her legs, and sank down.

"Oh." Her eyes were on him.

Connected. He felt his symbiont pulse, a rush of

feeling filling him. Heat, desire, caring. With a start, he realized it wasn't just his emotions alone. *Cren*. He was sensing Eve's emotions in the air as well, amplified by his helian.

Her eyes widened. "I can feel..."

"What I feel."

"Davion." She arched, coming again.

He lifted his hips up, powering inside her. *His. Them. Joined.* He couldn't form full thoughts, just felt all the churning emotions inside him.

"Come with me, baby." Her lips parted. "Come on me this time, on my skin."

He groaned, and as his orgasm hit, he pulled out of her. The warmth of his come splashed on her belly and his. He groaned again, seeing Eve touch the fluid.

Finally, she collapsed against him, the hammock still rocking. He turned his head and kissed her.

She made a humming noise. "That was..."

"Yes," he agreed.

After a few minutes, they roused enough to climb out of the hammock and head back to the small waterfall to clean up. Davion felt energized.

He found a cloth and cleaned off their skin. As he washed her belly, she smiled at him sleepily.

"Rest now, *shara*." He nudged her back into the hammock and followed her in.

"What's *shara* mean?"

"It's an endearment. What the warrior Alqin called his mate Eschar."

"Sounds pretty."

Pulling her close, Davion drifted off. But he was well

aware that the morning would come, and once again, they'd have to fight for their survival.

And now, for Davion, Eve's survival was more important to him than anything. His arms tightened. She was his and he would fight anyone in order to keep her by his side. Even his own people.

CHAPTER FIFTEEN

A night of rest and sex could work wonders.

Eve moved effortlessly through the long grass. Her body felt loose and limber. She was also filled with energy.

And raw determination. This time, she and Davion were the hunters.

The Kantos were the prey.

If they could find the bastards. So far, no sign of them. She let out a small growl.

"Good hunters are patient, Eve," Davion said.

She growled again. "You might have noticed that I won't be winning any medals for patience."

He grinned at her. God, when he grinned, he looked years younger. She grinned back. And damned if the war commander didn't look proud of her. Everyone else she knew had considered her boldness and impatience a detriment. Not Davion.

But when he jerked to a halt and straightened, her

happy feeling faded fast. He scanned the grass ahead, and she lifted her blasters.

"What?"

"We're being hunted."

A shiver worked down her spine. "Kantos?"

"Most likely." He moved closer. "Stay alert."

They jogged forward, the grass whispering in the light breeze. Overhead was a cloudless, blue sky, and not a starship to be seen.

They both knew that if Davion's message had made it through, his warriors should have been here by now.

She blew out a breath. One thing at a time. Take down the Kantos, then worry about getting off Hunter7.

Suddenly, a creature burst out of the long grass.

"Fuck." Eve stumbled back.

It looked like a giant praying mantis. Its hard shell was bright green, its upper body held upright. There were giant pincers at its gaping mouth, and it moved on six long, sturdy legs.

"What the hell is this one?" she called out.

The creature squawked, flattening the grass beneath it.

"A mantio," Davion said. "A bug the Kantos have bred to be killers. They're vicious and quick."

Why could the Kantos bugs never be cuddly and soft? She aimed one of her blasters, the autotargeting helping her line up the shot.

She fired and then Davion rushed forward, his sword forming on his arm. He slashed at the creature, and it reared back with a screech. Eve rushed in beside him, her own sword forming. Together, they pushed in, slashing and stabbing.

They fought together, darting in and out to fight the mantio.

Davion was right, the bug was fast. As sharp pincers rushed at Eve, she leaped back and spun.

As they fought, she noticed the creature's skin start to change color. She kept fighting, watching as the green turned to gold.

The next time she darted in, she was surprised by the wave of heat coming off it. Inside the mantio's belly, a shadow began to twist and move.

"Davion…"

"It's going to undergo metamorphosis. They usually shed their old skin and grow larger."

Shit. Enough. Eve snatched a small Eon grenade off her belt. She thumbed it and waited for the blue lights on it to flare. Then she ran a few steps, dodged one of the creature's legs, and slid in, feet-first, like she was coming in to home base.

She came in to land beneath the mantio. Reaching up, she slapped the grenade onto its skin.

It shrieked, and Eve turned, and rolled out from under it. Jumping up, she sprinted back toward Davion.

"Down!" She waved her arms. "Grenade."

He swung an arm around her and hauled her to the ground. They hit hard, the air rushing out of her. Then Davion crawled over her, covering her with his body.

The grenade exploded. Bits of dirt and clumps of grass landed near them, as well as chunks of… Well, she preferred not to focus on the chunks of bug.

Davion lifted his head and grimaced. "You're bloodthirsty."

She pressed a kiss to his jaw. "You love it."

He sighed. "I do."

The earth rumbled beneath them.

"Biome change." Davion helped her up.

They stood together, holding hands. "What now?"

Eve figured she should be used to it by this point, but when the ground started splitting open, her pulse still began to race. A crack opened up close to their boots, and they both backed up. She wondered what was next. She waited, expecting to see mountains rise into the sky or crazy vegetation spill out everywhere.

But nothing happened.

More cracks opened up, and she watched the grass shrivel up. She heard the sound of running water in the cracks.

"Oh, no," Davion murmured.

"Was that a good 'oh, no' or a bad 'oh, no'?"

"I believe there is only the bad kind in this place."

Water bubbled up out of the cracks.

Eve tilted her head. "Water? That doesn't seem too bad."

A giant gush rushed out of a large crack, washing up to their thighs. *Oh, shit*.

Another wave roared out of a large crack and crashed into them. It knocked them off their feet, and Eve found herself being rushed along the ground, like they were caught in a tidal wave.

She spat out some water and felt herself dropping.

Davion cursed, and they were washed over a ridge that hadn't been there moments before.

Splash.

They landed in water.

It closed over Eve's head and she kicked. Her head broke the surface, and she took a deep breath. She wiped the water from her eyes, treading water to stay afloat.

Davion was treading water beside her. "Aquatic biome."

Eve turned her head, her belly feeling like it had a coil of wire inside. She watched the last of the long grass disappear under the waves.

There was water as far she could see.

"Fucking great."

"We'll be fine." He touched her hair.

"Right. We have to swim, and who knows what the hell is below us."

Davion grimaced. "Probably best not to think of that."

"Now all I'm hearing is the *Jaws* theme tune."

He frowned. "Jaws?"

"Remind me to show you the movie sometime."

"I think I see land in that direction."

Eve squinted at the dark smudge. "Maybe."

"Time for a swim, my Earth warrior."

With a kick, Eve started out. Davion sliced easily through the water. Thankfully, the swells weren't too big.

"I wanted a beach, but this wasn't exactly what I was thinking," she muttered. "It would definitely be improved with an actual dry, sandy beach, and with drinks with little umbrellas in them."

Davion frowned. "You put umbrellas in drinks?"

"Never mind." Then she spotted something in the distance. She stopped, treading water. Something was on the water, moving in their direction

"Davion?"

He looked as well, a muscle ticking in his jaw. "Kantos."

She sighed. It was too much to ask that the bastards had drowned. The power-hungry aliens just kept coming.

As they got closer, she saw riders on water-skimming bugs. The bugs had long, narrow bodies and almost delicate legs that spread out, keeping them skimming above the water.

Eve knew they couldn't swim fast enough to outrun them. And—she looked around—they had nowhere to swim to.

Davion studied the incoming Kantos. "We're at a disadvantage."

"That's how the Kantos like it."

Moments later, they were surrounded by the water-skimming bugs and the soldiers riding them.

An Kantos elite moved closer. *War Commander Thann-Eon, we are here to get the codes you refused to give us last time.*

"Codes?" Eve whispered.

Davion's jaw tightened. "To the Eon warships. It's a backdoor code to take control of a ship's systems in the event of an emergency."

Eve blinked, then she started laughing. Then she laughed some more.

She saw confused looks on the faces of the Kantos.

What is so funny? Even in her head, the Kantos leader's tone sounded disgruntled.

"He'll *never* give you those codes. It doesn't matter what you do to him."

The Kantos leader glared at her.

"He's a freaking Eon warrior and a badass. There is no way."

The Kantos nodded. *We realize that.* Then he tilted his creepy head. *But perhaps what I do to you will convince him.*

Her chest locked. The Kantos soldier beside him shot something in Eve's direction.

The net clamped down around her, and the force of it knocked her down into the water. She came up sputtering, peering through the lattice of hard fibers that made up the net.

"Eve." Davion lunged for her, grabbing at the net. Their gazes met and she saw him lifting his arm, his sword forming.

Then the net was yanked violently through the water.

Shit.

It was a bumpy ride as she was dragged behind a Kantos skimmer. Her mouth kept filling with water and she spat it out, desperately trying to keep her head above the water.

They hit a wave and she went under. She kicked her legs, trying to hold her breath.

Her chest started to burn.

Shit. She struggled against the urge to breathe. The burn turned to an inferno. *No.*

Her mouth opened and water rushed in.

DAVION FELT a net brush past him and dodged to the side. He slashed out with his sword, cutting it to pieces.

Ahead, he watched the skimmer bug drag Eve through the water, doing a large circle around where Davion bobbed. They were drowning her.

The skimmer slowed and Eve's head, covered in the net, broke the surface.

"Eve!"

"Go!" she shouted before she was yanked under again.

Never. He wasn't going to leave her. Not like everyone in her life had before. He started swimming toward her.

He saw several Kantos lift projectile weapons, aiming at him. They fired and Davion dived beneath the water, kicking hard. He came up, not far from Eve. She was struggling against the net.

"I'm coming." He powered through the water and stretched out an arm. Their fingers brushed.

More projectiles hit the water, closer to him this time. They were harpoons.

"Watch out!" Eve screamed.

One projectile pierced Davion's shoulder. The burning shock almost knocked him under the surface. He gripped the spear sticking into him and yanked it out.

The skimmer Eve's net was tied to started moving again. Ignoring the blood and pain, Davion gripped the net with one hand. Then both he and Eve were being dragged across the water.

He was still gripping the harpoon in his other hand. Pulling his arm back, he waited for the wild ride to smooth out a little, then tossed it.

The spear hit the soldier in the neck, knocking him off the bug. Riderless, the bug rocketed forward, turned in a confused circle, then finally slowed to a stop.

"Eve." Davion gripped her the best he could through the net and hauled her up.

He had to free her.

"They're coming," she choked out.

He looked over his shoulder. The other Kantos skimmers were closing in.

"I'll get you free." He shrugged out of his backpack—it was weighing him down. He moved to cut the net, but the Kantos skimmer moved, yanking her away, almost out of his grasp.

Cren. He gripped the net more firmly, and started cutting through the tough fibers.

More projectiles sailed through the air. Davion ducked down, and the harpoons missed them.

Instead, they peppered the skimmer. It let out a mournful cry and slumped in the water.

"They're stopping us from getting away," Eve said.

Davion gritted his teeth and went back to cutting the net. It was so damn tough.

Eve spat out some water, dropping lower in the water. "Davion."

She was being dragged under. That's when he realized that the dead skimmer bug was sinking, and it was taking the net and Eve with it.

No. He cut harder.

Eve thrashed, trying to keep her head above water. "Leave me, Davion. They're almost here. Go before they catch you."

"No." Despair tore at his chest.

"Davion, more than just our lives are at stake."

"I said no," he roared.

He heard the clicking sounds of the Kantos. They were close.

"Go." Her fingers brushed his. "Find your people and make the Kantos pay."

He dragged her close, kissing her through the net. "I can't do that. I can't leave you."

"You're the strongest man I know. True to the core." Her voice broke. "You can do anything."

Pain ripped him to shreds. "Eve—"

They were both dragged under a wave. He swallowed water and kicked hard. They both sucked in air and spat out some water.

"Save my planet, Davion. Promise me."

He tried to pull her up, but even all his enhanced strength wasn't enough to lift her, the net, and the dead skimmer bug.

"Promise me," she said again.

"I promise."

Her face smoothed out. "Thank you."

A fierce surge of emotion choked his throat. "I can't leave you."

The Kantos' clicking increased. They were almost on

top of them. Only Eve's nose and lips were above the waterline.

"Go, my war commander."

Then she slipped beneath the water. Davion dived under and heaved. He fought the heavy drag, refusing to give up. He saw Eve thrashing, desperate for air, and soon his own lungs were ablaze. *Come on.*

Calling on every bit of strength he and his helian had, he surged up. He heaved in air and heard Eve spluttering.

But he could feel the weight dragging on her again. Relentless.

A giant splash sounded from somewhere nearby. An aquatic creature leaped out of the waves. It had sleek, gray skin, and a long, stream-lined body. It swam up, bumping into Davion.

Cren. He pushed the animal away.

"Go," she whispered.

The creature circled around, cutting through the water fast. It circled around them again, and as it did, Eve slipped completely beneath the water.

"No!" Davion heaved on the edge of the net, trying to pull her up.

The water creature nudged him away from Eve. Reflexively, Davion grabbed the fin on top of the creature to stay afloat.

The animal shot away, swimming so fast water sprayed up into Davion's face.

No. "Eve!" His roar echoed across the water.

He looked back, and watched the Kantos circle the spot where she'd gone down. There was no sign of her. She'd been taken by the waves.

CHAPTER SIXTEEN

Davion coughed up water, his lungs burning. The aquatic animal gave him a hard shove. He flew through the water and landed on sand.

Coming up on his hands and knees, he vomited up more water. The gentle waves lapped at him, and he knew the sound should be soothing. It wasn't.

He raised his head in an attempt to get his bearings. He was on an island. There was a long beach consisting of yellow sand, and a wall of thick vegetation, including tall trees with spiral trunks.

There was also a health station on the sand. He rose, intent on heading up to the metallic dome, trying not to think.

Trying not to let the emotional agony inside him rip him to shreds.

He heard a splash, and swiveled. The aquatic creature was in the shallows, swimming in circles. It had a sleek, gray body, several fins, an elongated snout, and very sharp teeth.

It splashed playfully at him, using its tail to spray water onto the sand.

"Go away," Davion snarled.

The creature had taken him from Eve.

The animal splashed again, and Davion looked more closely. Bright aqua eyes.

He stilled. "Shaggy?"

More happy splashing.

Davion felt a burst of something in his chest. He splashed knee-deep into the water, sliding his palm along Shaggy's rubbery side.

By Eschar's bow, Eve would be thrilled. *Eve*. Davion's hands clenched on Shaggy.

Blue-green eyes looked up at him. "We need to find Eve, boy."

But dark thoughts pounded inside Davion's head. She'd been dragged beneath the water. *Gone*. He'd been helpless to save her. He sucked in a breath.

She was likely dead, and that thought ripped him inside and left him bleeding. If the Kantos had saved her…then she was their prisoner.

He bowed his head.

Either way, he was bringing the woman he loved home. *Love. His mate. His other half.*

Eve Traynor of Earth was the woman who'd been made for him. He *wasn't* leaving her.

Turning, he strode to the health station. Methodically, he squeezed havv onto his wounds and pressed a stim to his neck. He shot himself with another dose. He'd exceeded the dosage and it was dangerous, but worth the risk.

Energy rushed through his veins. Determination rocketed through him. Eve had saved him, over and over. She'd never given up on him.

Now he was going to save her, and then, together, they'd save her planet.

Davion needed weapons. He'd lost his wrist screen, but there was a small screen in the health station. He tapped on it and a map appeared.

There. There was a weapon's cache not too far away.

But as he turned his head in the cache's direction, he realized that he was looking at the water.

Cren. The cache was underwater. *Wonderful.*

He strode back into the water, giving a sharp whistle. Shaggy appeared with a splash.

"We're going to get Eve, boy." Another splash. "But first we need to get to the weapons cache."

Reaching out, Davion gripped Shaggy's top fin and waded farther into the water.

"Go, Shaggy. Dive."

They tore through the water and Davion dragged in a deep breath. And then Shaggy dived beneath the waves.

The water was a clear, crystalline blue. As they went deeper, Davion saw a huge school of fish of all shapes, sizes and colors. They scattered around like dancing butterflies.

They cut through the water like an arrow, and in the distance, he saw the shadow of a giant creature moving slowly through the ocean.

Davion didn't care what he faced. He was only focused on Eve and getting her back.

They moved along the bottom of the sandy sea floor and hit some long strands of green vegetation, waving in the current. He pulled himself in close to Shaggy, careful not to get tangled.

His lungs started to burn, but he held his breath.

Was this how Eve felt when she was dragged under? He gripped Shaggy harder, and just as his lungs were reaching breaking point, he saw the glimmer of a blue dome ahead.

Shaggy swam right up to the dome and Davion let go. With a powerful kick, he swam to the dome entrance and pressed his palm to the lock.

Quickly, he tumbled inside. He was in a small vestibule. The door closed behind him and the water drained out. Heaving in air, he staggered through the main door into the cache.

Stumbling, he sat on a crate. He pulled in more deep breaths. The entire dome was clear, and he had a perfect view of the water around him, and the wildlife swimming past.

Pushing his wet hair out of his face, he studied the weapons locker in the center of the dome. Standing, he moved over and opened it. Then he started yanking out grenades and weapons.

He slotted grenades into his belt, knives into sheaths that his armor created for him, and a blaster over his back.

Once he had enough, he stood and took a deep breath. Outside the dome, he saw Shaggy turning circles, ready and eager.

It was time to find Eve and get her back.

It would only be her body—pain tore at him, his throat raw—but he didn't care. He wouldn't abandon his mate.

He headed for the exit. When he swam out into the water, he gripped Shaggy again.

The animal didn't seem to need any directions. He powered through the water, taking Davion with him, heading up to the surface.

Eve. Davion looked at the glimmer of light ahead. *I'm coming, my Earth warrior.*

BUBBLES STREAMED around Eve's face. Her chest aching, she struggled hard.

The claws gripping her hair pulled and her face was yanked out of the water. She gasped, sucking in air.

I can keep doing this all day, Terran.

God, she hated that creepy, raspy voice in her head. The Kantos had pulled her out of the ocean and revived her, only to try to drown her again.

She lifted her hand and shot the Kantos the finger.

He dunked her under again, holding her until her mouth opened and water flooded in.

Fuck. It hurt. And she was getting tired. Fear and panic clawed at her insides, but she fought it down.

He yanked her out of the water again, and she heaved in a breath.

They were on a gorgeous beach somewhere. In the trees behind them, insects were chirping, and birds were calling. And in front of her, the beautiful, blue ocean stretched out to the horizon.

She'd been stripped of her gear and weapons. They hadn't noticed the scales circling her wrist…and she wasn't going to draw attention to the piece of Davion's helian.

Clicking filled her head. *Where is the war commander?*

"Preparing to kick your ass."

The Kantos dunked her head under again.

As she flailed in the water, she thought of Davion. God, she hoped he was okay. She had no idea what had happened to him, but at least the Kantos didn't have him.

Just picturing Davion's strong, rugged face calmed her. *Davion.* Her warrior. Her lover. Her man.

He'd left her and this time, she was glad. She wanted him to be safe, to live. She realized now that she truly loved him. He was her match in every way. She wished… wished they'd had more time together.

The Kantos held her under a bit longer this time and when he lifted her head, she was limp and tired. She coughed up water. She'd lost track of how many times he'd dunked her.

"He'll make you pay." Her voice was scratchy and water-logged. "You kill me, you'll ignite his need for vengeance. The full might of the Eon and Earth will come down on you." Well, maybe not, but it sounded good.

The Kantos snorted. *The Eon detest the Terrans. And there is nothing mightier than the Kantos.*

"That's where you're wrong. Very, very wrong."

Eve blinked at the deep voice. *Davion's* voice. She must be hallucinating.

But the Kantos turned, yanking her with him. Eve lifted her head, she saw Davion striding out of the water like some sea god.

Her heart clenched. *No.* There were too many Kantos for him to take on alone. The macho idiot.

The Kantos holding her straightened. *Kill him!*

The Kantos soldiers swarmed Davion. But he charged into the melee, exploding into action—spinning, hitting, and kicking. His blue sword swung through the air, vicious and deadly.

Eve saw green Kantos blood spray on the sand.

Davion lobbed some grenades and they exploded, sand flying into the air, along with screeching Kantos. He powered through the fighters, blade swinging. Unstoppable. A force of nature.

The alien holding Eve pulled her up, holding her like a shield. She could barely touch the ground. She swung her elbows, trying to fight him, but after the repeated near drownings, her moves were sluggish and uncoordinated.

Davion went down on one knee, tossing a grenade with an underarm throw. It hit the sand, rolled, and exploded. This one sprayed a sticky blue-green substance that splattered the Kantos. The clicking sounds and screeches exploded in a fever pitch that hurt Eve's ears.

The Kantos elite holding her swung her around, one hard arm across her chest. She felt a blade pressed against her throat.

Stop, War Commander, or your toy is dead.

Davion paused, glaring.

"Toy?" Eve said.

That is all that could ever be between a Terran and an Eon.

Davion's eyes blazed, all of it focused on her and the Kantos. God, he was something. Eve's belly flooded. There was so much emotion in his eyes but the Kantos just couldn't comprehend it.

"You are so wrong, bug boy," Eve said.

Really?

"Yes." Davion threw out one powerful arm.

Black cascaded off his armor, flowing through the air like smoke. It hit Eve's chest.

The Kantos made a shocked sound, but Eve stood still, absorbing the symbiont.

It flowed over her skin. She felt warmth wash though her, and power infuse her system. Scale armor formed on her body, molding to her.

Then she grinned and ducked, pulling away from the stunned Kantos.

As the alien leaped back, Eve imagined a sword and it formed on her arm. She rushed him, his yellow gaze on her.

"Not a toy." She strode toward him and he backed up.

Davion moved into view. He charged at the other Kantos, his sword glowing as he cut through them.

Eve smiled. Magnificent, and all hers.

The Kantos elite in front of her threw his arms out. The clicking sound intensified—desperate and afraid. *Torax. Use the torax.*

Eve swung her sword. He dodged. She launched at him and he threw up his armored arm to block her hits.

I'm coming for you, asshole. She was taking this bastard down.

Nearby, a Kantos soldier scrambled out of the fight. He yanked what looked like a small cocoon off his back. He dropped it onto the sand, and the water lapped at it.

The cocoon immediately began to swell.

What the hell?

Around her, many of the Kantos fighters started to back away. She felt a nervous energy flow over the beach.

The cocoon kept growing. Soon, it was the size of a car. *Hell.*

She slashed at the Kantos leader, scoring him across his chest. He hissed and fell to the ground.

"Eve." Davion appeared, grabbing her arm.

She touched his chest. "Nice to see you, warrior."

He stroked his fingers along her jaw. "I thought I'd lost you."

"Right here, Dav." She moved her hand to his and squeezed. "And pretty damned happy about it, even if I'm pissed you came back."

He smiled. "You've rubbed off on me."

Together, they turned to look at the growing cocoon. It was now the size of a shuttle.

"What is this?" she asked.

"I've never seen it before, but it must be some new Kantos weapon. I'm guessing it's something bad."

Eve rolled her eyes. "You are the king of understatement."

The cocoon burst. Scaly legs broke free, and whatever was inside let out a fierce, high-pitched scream.

Torax. The raspy voice echoed in their heads. *The ultimate weapon.*

The giant, black bug pulled itself free of the cocoon. It had scaled legs, giant pincers, and a huge, scorpion-like stinger that reared up above its head. A row of hungry, brilliant-blue eyes zeroed in on them.

"Not good," Eve said.

The Kantos monster let out another God-awful screech. One of its legs came crashing down, causing the ground to shake under the impact.

"Now who is the king of understatement?" Davion said.

They both raised their weapons. She looked at him. "Ready to fight?"

His sword pulsed with light. "Always, my Earth warrior."

Together, they rushed forward.

CHAPTER SEVENTEEN

Sweat dripped down Davion's face. He swung his sword, hit the creature's scaled leg, then quickly rolled out of the way.

No effect.

He cursed under his breath. He and Eve had been attacking it again and again, and they weren't making a dent in the cursed thing.

The creature's stinger rushed at him, and Davion dived out of the way.

Eve leaped over his head, her sword raised in the air. She sliced at the alien monster, her blade scoring along its side.

It left a mark on the scales, but not much. The sword had barely penetrated.

They'd been fighting for what felt like hours, and they were having no impact.

The Kantos beast stomped on some vegetation. With a screech, its stinger slammed down amongst some

Kantos soldiers. It was hungry, fierce, and out-of-control. It didn't care who it attacked.

It was covered in black scales identical to the one that formed Davion's helian armor.

The torax swiveled its head, focusing on Eve and Davion. Hungry, mindless eyes burned into them. Blue eyes the same color as Davion's sword. It was a creature bred to hunt and kill.

The Kantos had, at some time, clearly stolen a helian. They'd experimented on it, corrupted it, and created this monster.

Rage poured through his veins like molten lava. They'd taken something sacred and abused it, using it to bring this abomination into existence.

Davion pulled his last grenade off his belt. "Eve, get back." He tossed a grenade at the creature.

She sprinted back toward him. He saw the stinger swinging at her.

"Watch out!"

It hit the ground right behind her feet. The dirt exploded beneath her and tossed her in the air. Then, the grenade exploded.

Eve flew through the air, arms and legs flailing. Then she hit the ground hard, as the explosion tossed rocks, sand, and trees into the air.

Davion ran to her. When he reached her, she was already up on one knee, but looked dazed.

"You okay?" he asked.

She licked her lips. "Okay. May have cracked a few ribs." Pain crossed her face.

The Kantos creature reared, letting out a harsh

screech. The stinger came down again, smashing into rock nearby. It was pulverized under the force of the blow.

Then the beast opened its massive jaws and some sort of blue liquid sprayed out of its maw.

"Oh, hell."

Davion knocked Eve to the ground. He felt the fluid splatter his armor and heard a sizzle.

Then a burning, stinging feeling rocked through him.

"What's happening?" Eve sat up, eyes wide.

Davion slapped at his armor. His symbiont was in pain. The poison was burning holes *through* his armor.

He gritted his teeth. Patches of his skin were visible in places. His armor had been eaten away.

He looked over and saw the Kantos soldiers smiling.

"Poison. Designed to debilitate my symbiont."

"Fuckers." Eve raised her weapon. "They'll regret it."

Davion stared at her, feeling his world shift. She was his everything. He nodded and raised his own sword.

"We need to attack the stinger," she said. "Together."

"Together."

They rushed forward together. The stinger crashed down again. They both leaped toward it, swords flashing in the sunlight.

Davion elongated his sword, pinning the stinger to the sand. The creature thrashed, and Eve stabbed and slashed it.

It screeched wildly, green blood soaking into the sand. Its legs moved onto less stable sand, and it tilted precariously.

"Drive it back," Davion cried.

He yanked his sword free, and they both charged the creature. The injured stinger was bent at an odd angle, and the monster seemed confused.

It scuttled backward, farther into the water.

"Keep going," Eve yelled.

There was a splash in the shallows. Davion spotted Shaggy. He leaped into the air, before knifing back into the water. Similar aquatic animals splashed with him. An entire pack of them.

"Drive it toward Shaggy," Davion said.

"Shaggy?"

"He's alive. An aquatic creature now."

Eve grinned and spun her weapon. They drove the Kantos creature deeper into the water, the waves lapping at it.

Shaggy darted forward, nipping at the softer underbelly. The creature roared, legs splashing in the water.

Davion morphed his symbiont into a blaster weapon. It hurt. His symbiont was in pain, but it obeyed. He aimed the blaster at the creature's head and fired.

Boom. Boom.

The creature screeched, half collapsing in the water.

Eve laughed at Davion. "God, you are badass. Is it wrong that I want to jump you right now?"

His woman. Davion just shook his head.

From behind, he heard the enraged clicking of the Kantos soldiers.

Cren. Taking on a fresh wave of soldiers was the last thing he and Eve needed. He could see her arm hanging by her side, and his symbiont was still writhing in agony.

A boom echoed in the sky and Davion's gut clenched.

By Ston's sword, more Kantos reinforcements. Eve cursed.

But when he glanced up, elation burst through his exhaustion.

They were ships from the *Desteron*.

"Your guys?"

"Yes."

"Man, they have crappy timing." Her nose wrinkled. "An hour or two earlier would have been better. We've saved the day all by ourselves. Now they'll want to share the credit."

Davion barked out a laugh.

The Kantos beast thrashed in the water. Shaggy and his friends were busy tearing it to pieces. Hearing more splashing sounds, Davion turned. The last of the soldiers were sprinting toward them.

He opened fire with his blaster. When a few got too close, Eve sailed in, her sword a dangerous blur. Soon, the aquamarine water was tinged with green.

Eve lowered her sword, a smile lighting up her face. "I hope you have a big bed on your warship, warrior."

"I'm the war commander. Of course, I do." He couldn't wait to have her in it, spread out on his sheets.

The Kantos beast suddenly reared up out of the water with an ear-piercing roar. Not dead yet.

He scowled and heard Eve curse. They both spun.

The giant, damaged stinger rushed forward. It hit the water, then rose high into the air again.

"Damn thing doesn't know it's dead." Eve turned toward Davion.

All of a sudden, the stinger stabbed down. It rammed

into Eve, piercing through her stomach and pinning her to the sand.

Davion froze, his arms falling to his sides. Eve's blue eyes were wide and shocked. She looked down at her stomach and the large stinger sticking into her belly. Blood was rapidly beginning to pool around the wound.

"No!" Davion roared. He fired wildly on the beast.

Eve coughed and a trickle of blood ran out of her mouth. The stinger retracted, and the dead alien sank into the water.

Eve collapsed back and Davion raced to her. He fell to his knees, pulling her into his arms.

No. No. No. "Eve!"

He paid no attention to Shaggy's pack tearing the beast apart. He focused entirely on his wounded mate.

His symbiont linked them and he felt her pain, felt her stuttering heart and ragged breaths. He kept his gaze locked on Eve's face. His dying mate's face.

THROUGH THE FOG OF PAIN, Eve heard a voice talking—urgent and fierce.

It was telling her to hold on.

But there was so much pain. She felt hands pressing down on her belly and she cried out.

"Eve, look at me. Look at me, *shara*."

Her eyelids felt so heavy, but through sheer grit, she managed to pry them open. She stared into Davion's handsome, ravaged face.

Her Davion.

"Eve, hold on. *Promise* me."

She tried to talk but no sound came out. Her eyes started to drift closed...

"No. Keep them open."

His voice snapped them open again and she tried to focus on him. She saw the lines bracketing his mouth. He was in pain. He was hurt, too.

He lurched to his feet, carrying her. But they hadn't gone far when he dropped to his knees with a groan, his breathing harsh. He fell on his side, but he held her close. The water lapped at them.

Eve slipped in and out of consciousness. She had no idea how much time passed, but again she heard deep voices. More than one.

"Aydin, he's injured. See to him. The war commander is our priority."

Eve was wrenched away roughly from Davion and she cried out in pain. Nausea washed through her.

"Davion," a masculine voice said.

She cracked open an eye. Davion was passed out beside her, and towering over them was a tall man in Eon armor. He cast a shadow over Eve.

Another armored man knelt beside Davion, a scanner held over his body. A doctor or medic.

Davion jerked awake. "No. Eve. See to her. She's hurt bad."

"We're helping you first," the standing warrior said.

Eve couldn't manage any words. She saw red blood staining the water and knew it was hers. Weakness was spreading through her limbs.

"No! Brack, see to Eve." Davion shrugged the doctor off him. "Aydin, help her!"

"But she's…Terran," the doctor said.

"She abducted you," the other man said incredulously. "We managed to decrypt the mess she made of our security feed. We saw her drag your unconscious body onto your shuttle."

"Help her," Davion roared. "She's mine. She's my mate."

Then Davion was close, his face near hers, his hands pressing against her wound. "I'm here, *shara*."

But Eve had no strength left to reassure him.

"Eve, hold on." He looked down at her. "*Cren*, there's so much blood."

"Out of my way." The doctor, Aydin, dominated her view. She had no idea what he was doing but she felt warmth, and then the pain was gone.

Now she felt cold.

"Dav—"

"I'm here, my courageous Earth warrior. I'm here."

"Cold."

His face spasmed. "Hold on."

Then she felt like she was shaking.

"*Cren*," someone cried out. "The biome is changing. Secure the war commander—"

"Hold on, Eve."

She wanted to, but a yawning black hole opened up in front of her. She tried to fight it, tried to stay with Davion.

But the hole swallowed her. Her eyelids closed, and then there was nothing.

CHAPTER EIGHTEEN

Eve opened her eyes and blinked.

She was lying on a bed, and there was no sound, no pain, nothing. She turned her head. A number of tubes were running out of her body to several machines. The lines were filled with red and blue fluids.

She frowned. A medical ward. Actually, it looked like the med ward on the Citadel Prison. She blinked again. Yep, it was the prison infirmary.

Her pulse kicked into gear and a machine beeped like crazy. Memories hit her like laser blasts.

Hunter7.

The Kantos.

Abducting Davion. *Davion.*

Being injured.

She shoved the sheet back and touched her belly. She only found smooth skin. Her essentials were covered by a few white strips of fabric—typical attire for medical treatment.

She looked around again. Yes, definitely the Citadel Prison.

Her gut went hard. God, had it all been a dream? Her heart started pounding. Was she still on Citadel? Had she hallucinated everything? *No.* Panic burned through her.

Davion couldn't have been a dream. Not everything they'd been through, everything they'd shared.

Everything she felt for him. She loved him and that was real, *dammit*.

She sat up, ignoring the throb in her head. She shoved off the bed, wavered for a second, then started ripping the tubes off. Alarms blared.

A few tubes wouldn't come free of her skin, so she tore them out of the machines instead. She staggered toward the door, trailing the tubes behind her.

The walls shimmered for a second and she frowned, but she focused her gaze on the door.

She wanted Davion. She wanted his strong arms around her, his strength supporting her.

The door whispered open and she lurched out into the corridor. Dizziness hit her, and she squeezed her eyes shut. She pressed a palm to the wall to hold herself up.

She opened her eyes and frowned. Out here looked nothing like the Citadel Prison.

Confusion rushed through Eve. *What the hell was going on?*

A big man appeared at the end of the corridor, striding toward her. Another wave of dizziness hit her, and she worried that she was about to fall. But she kept watching the tall, broad-shouldered man.

"Davion," she whispered.

As the man drew closer, she saw it wasn't Davion. Disappointment flooded her. He was big and muscled, with long hair that didn't quite reach his shoulders, but not Davion. His eyes had strands of grass-green in them.

She sagged. "Where am I?"

"Are you trying to set your recovery back?" The man scowled at her, looking pissed. He reached for her.

Eve lurched back. "Who...where...?" Dammit, her head was so foggy. All she wanted was Davion. "Where's Davion?"

"You need to get back into bed—" The man reached for her again.

Eve acted on instinct. She ducked low, spinning under the man's arm. She whipped one of the attached tubes into her hand. Then she wrapped it around her attacker's neck.

He jerked in surprise. Standing behind him, Eve kicked at his knees, knocking his legs out from under him.

He grunted and twisted, moving fast. The man might be some kind of a doctor, but he was still a warrior.

Eve pressed a knee into his back and pulled the tube back. "Please answer my questions, and don't touch me."

"Eve."

A familiar deep voice. She dropped the tube and turned unsteadily.

There was Davion.

Warmth burst to life inside her. He was running down the corridor toward her, his big body powering fast.

Everything inside her expanded and flared. *Davion.* He was here. It hadn't been a dream.

A sob broke free from her throat and she took two steps toward him. Then her legs collapsed.

She didn't hit the floor. Davion leaped the last few meters, catching her and pulling her close.

"I woke up..." She knew her voice sounded panicked. "It looked like the prison where I'd been held. I thought you and everything that happened were a dream—"

"Shh. I'm here. We're very much alive and real."

She buried her hands in his hair, pressing her forehead to his. She breathed him in, that dark scent she loved.

"I've got you," he murmured. "Always. Never leaving you, *shara*."

Eve burrowed closer, like she could get under his skin.

"I'm sorry, Davion," a deep voice said from behind them. "I thought familiar surroundings would soothe her and did a hologram of her most recent memories."

"It's fine, Aydin." Davion dropped his head and pressed his mouth to hers.

When he pulled back, Eve glanced at the doctor. He was still on his knees, rubbing his red throat. *Whoops.*

"Aydin, are you injured?" Davion asked.

"I'm fine," the doctor growled, lurching to his feet.

"Um...sorry about that," Eve said.

Both men's gazes swung to her. A smile flirted on Davion's lips and he just shook his head.

Running footsteps. Another warrior arrived.

"Everything is okay, Brack," Davion assured the newcomer.

Brack raised a brow. "You're sure? Aydin looks like he

went a round with Caze in the gym, and you are clutching a Terran like she's the meaning of the universe. That doesn't shout 'everything is okay' to me."

"I like him," Eve murmured.

"You would," Davion said. "Eve, this is my second-in-command, Second Commander Brack Thann-Felis and my Medical Commander, Aydin Kann-Ath. Warriors, this is Sub-Captain Eve Traynor."

The men nodded.

Davion cupped her face. "Are you okay, Eve?"

"I'm fine. My injury is healed."

Suddenly, Davion's symbiont pulsed and she felt it. There were no words, just feelings, but she knew it was checking that she was okay. She reached out and stroked the band on his wrist.

The symbiont pulsed up her arm, black scales covering her skin.

He pulled her closer. "I was so afraid." A near-silent whisper.

God, her warrior. She gripped him tightly.

Brack and Aydin both made strangled noises. They stared at Eve like she were a Kantos creature that had just burst out of an egg.

"It...your helian, it responds to her?" Aydin choked out.

Davion nodded.

"You should have told me! It would have changed my healing protocols." Clearly recovering from his shock, the doctor moved closer, pressing his fingers to Eve's neck.

"Uh, touching me didn't work out so well for you last time," she said.

The warrior froze, green-black eyes flicking to hers. "I'm...sorry. May I check your vitals?"

"Sure."

An excited *woof* echoed in the corridor. Eve lifted her head and saw a medium-sized, brown-and-white canine running toward them. It reached them, wiggled its butt, and then bumped its head against Eve. It lifted its woolly head and familiar aqua eyes stared at Eve.

"Shaggy?" Warmth exploded inside her.

"I brought him with us," Davion said.

"For some *Cren*-cursed reason." Brack's face twisted. "The creature is a menace."

"The biome changed just before we left Hunter7," Davion added. "He went from aquatic animal to this."

"Hey, boy." Shaggy licked her face and gave a yip. Eve laughed.

"Aydin, how is she?" Davion demanded.

"Fine. Healed and healthy. She needs more rest, however. But in light of your symbiont's reaction to her, I think it would be better if she stays with you."

Davion nodded, rising and taking Eve into his arms. "You can remove the last of these tubes?"

"Yes."

"Good. Do it. Then if you need us, we'll be in my cabin."

DAVION CARRIED Eve to his cabin, laying her down gently on his bed. "You need to rest."

Shaggy, who'd already made a bed in Davion's closet, trotted to his spot and disappeared through the doors.

Eve looked around and smiled. "This is where we first met."

"Where you abducted me?"

She grinned. "Sure did. You were gloriously naked."

"Impertinent female." He plumped the pillows behind her. She looked gorgeous. Her skin was glowing, and there was no sign of her grievous injury.

His gut tightened. He hated the memory of her so badly hurt. "Now, time to rest."

"No." She grabbed his arms.

"Eve—"

"I need you."

He hesitated.

Her fingers tightened. "Please."

He slid in beside her, wrapping himself around her. She nuzzled close and he breathed in her scent. He closed his eyes for a second and memories peppered him. He'd come so close to losing her.

A shudder ran through him. Eve turned her head, her lips pressing against his collarbone. Then her hands started unfastening his shirt.

He groaned. "You need to rest. Doctor's orders."

She smiled at him. "I've never been that great with orders. When have we ever actually rested?" She shoved his shirt off. "I need skin."

Davion let her divest him of his shirt. Her hands stroked over his skin, hunger flaring in her eyes. He pushed her back on the bed, ripping her medical outfit off. Then she was naked, and he set his mouth on her. He kissed her all over—neck, breasts, belly, thighs—until she was writhing. He worshipped her, checking every inch of her skin.

He lavished her belly with attention. It would take a long time for him to forget what had happened to her. But thankfully, Aydin was good at his job, and there was no sign of her wound.

Eve twisted, rearing up. She shoved Davion down on the sheets, and then her mouth was on him.

She took her time. Nipping at his skin, sucking his nipples, tongue tracing over the ridges of his stomach. When she sucked his cock into her mouth, he bucked.

Soon, he couldn't stand it anymore. He wasn't coming in her mouth. He wanted to come inside her tight body.

Davion rose up on his knees and gripped her waist, lifting her. She smiled, wrapping her legs around his hips. He jerked her down, plunging inside her.

He gritted his teeth. So good. He watched the look on her face. Could watch her forever.

"You're always wet and ready for me," he growled.

"Yes."

They kissed again, as he continued driving inside her. It didn't take long until her cries changed, became more urgent.

"Come, my Earth warrior. My mate."

Her orgasm hit her and her head dropped back with a scream.

Driven by the need to find the release only Eve could give him, Davion kept thrusting inside her. More. Deeper.

Then he pulled out of her, listening to her cry of protest. He spun her onto her hands and knees.

He covered her, pressing one hand to the bed, his cock into her tight heat.

She turned her head to look at him, and he saw that her eyes were burning, glowing a neon blue that matched the filaments in his eyes.

He realized what was happening. An Eon mating fever. A cementing of their union, powered by the amplification of their feelings by his symbiont.

He looked up and saw their reflection in the mirror on the closet. Her face was flushed, and his body looked almost brutal covering her smaller form.

But the sight made him harder. He'd never seen anything sexier. He shifted a hand beneath Eve, sliding his hand across her skin, until he stroked the top of her folds. He found her clit, rolling it between his fingers.

She bucked. "Hell, yes."

"So beautiful."

"You're beautiful," she gasped.

He pinched her clit and her back arched. "Find it again, Eve."

"With you, it's guaranteed."

Davion felt his own release gathering, and felt a pulse from his symbiont.

"Oh," she cried out. "That feels *so* amazing."

He'd heard stories of the mating fever, but he'd never felt anything close to this. With his symbiont amplifying their emotions, he felt the exact moment when she came. He experienced the rush of scorching pleasure she felt, and it set off his orgasm.

Pistoning into her, he groaned through the gut-wrenching pleasure.

Together they collapsed, covered in sweat. He felt his release leaking down her leg, but she just smiled lazily.

"I believe we're experiencing an Eon mating fever."

She blinked. "Say again."

"The helian amplifies our desires. It helps cement a mating."

"A fuck-a-thon?" She ran her tongue over her teeth. "Sounds good to me."

"It can last several days."

Her mouth dropped open. "Days?" Then she smiled wickedly. "I'm game."

He smiled in response. "Shower?"

"Can't move. You go." She waved a hand.

He nuzzled her. "Did I tire out my Earth warrior?"

"Give me a second, and I'll recover enough to take you on."

He kissed her shoulder. "I didn't hurt you?"

"Not even close."

"The mating fever can be intense."

"I abducted the most fearsome Eon war commander and battled waves of Kantos on a killer planet. An Eon mating fever with the sexiest man I know?" She made a *pfft* sound. "Piece of cake."

That was his Eve. "In case it wasn't obvious, I love you, Eve Traynor."

Emotions flitted across her face. "In case it wasn't obvious, Davion Thann-Eon, I love you, too."

Just hearing her say the words had elation flowing

through him. He kissed her again. "You're my perfect match. I think my symbiont knew it before me."

"Clever alien organism." Then her face turned serious. She shoved her mussed hair back. "But what now, warrior?"

"What do you mean?"

She sat up. "You're an Eon war commander and I'm a Terran criminal. Your people hate mine. And the Kantos—"

"Shh." He gripped her chin. "We'll face it together. All of it. We make a hell of a team, and we can tackle anything. Disapproving people and killer aliens are nothing."

She smiled. "True."

"I'll fight anything and anyone to stay at your side."

She bit her lip. "If you make me cry, I'll hit you."

"Well, if you're feeling refreshed." He lowered his head, pressing a kiss to one breast.

She squirmed beneath him. "I'm still a bit tired. You'll have to do all the work."

"It will be my pleasure, my mate."

CHAPTER NINETEEN

Eve sensed movement and cracked open one eye.

Aydin was beside the bed, running a scanner over her. She jerked, yanking the sheet up. God, she was naked. The twisted sheet was only preserving the barest hint of her modesty.

Davion was facedown beside her and completely out.

"What are you doing here?" Her voice was husky with sleep.

"Checking you're both alive."

She sat up on the pillows, clutching the sheet to her breasts. She gave a small groan. She and Davion had pretty much had sex for two days straight. She was more than a little achy.

"We're alive," she muttered.

"I'm told the mating fever can be…intense."

She snorted. "You don't say."

A faint smile crossed the doctor's rugged face. His scanner beeped. "The only thing you need right now is some sustenance." He aimed the scanner at Davion. "As does your mate."

Stirring, Davion groaned and rolled. His gaze snagged on Aydin and he scowled.

The doctor held up his hands. "I was the unlucky one selected to invade your cabin." He paused. "And to inform you that the king has requested you contact him."

Davion's face cleared. "When?"

"In twenty ship minutes."

Davion cursed, threw the covers back, and pushed out of the bed. Apparently, he wasn't fazed being naked in front of his warrior. Eve blatantly watched his ass as he headed for the washroom.

"I'll be ready," Davion called back.

Aydin cleared his throat. "He wants to see Eve, as well."

Eve rubbed her suddenly sweaty palms on the sheets. *Shit.*

"He's extremely interested in the Terran sent to abduct you. The same Terran you mated."

Davion nodded from the washroom doorway. "We'll see you on the bridge."

As soon as the doctor left, Eve ran for the shower. God, she needed to be presentable to meet a king. The freaking king of the Eon Empire.

When she looked in the mirror, she nearly screamed. Her hair was a tangled mess and she had a large hickey on the side of her neck. She spun. Davion was turning on the shower and when she saw his back, she winced. He had several scratch marks down his skin and a matching hickey on his neck. Yikes. Two of them.

"Come on, my Earth warrior." He nudged her into the misty shower. "Surely you aren't afraid."

"I'm not afraid…exactly."

But as they showered and dressed, Eve felt her nerves growing. Her entire planet and all the people on it depended on her talking the king into supporting them. Hand in hand, they headed out into the corridor.

The bridge doors approached and she blew out a breath. She'd prefer to be facing down a swarm of Kantos. Davion squeezed her fingers.

"It will be fine," he said.

"I've never met a king."

"He recently accepted the mantle from his father. Gayel is a good man."

Right. Who'd had his war commander abducted and tossed into danger by the very people who needed his help.

They strode onto the bridge and she felt every single warrior look at them. Nearby, Brack looked at them with amusement. Of course, the man's gaze went straight to the bruises she'd left on Davion's neck. Eve wanted to wither, but Davion straightened and smiled. Like he was proud, or something. She wanted to smack him, but instead, fought her threatening blush.

"We've made connection with the palace, War Commander," a young warrior called out.

Davion nodded. "Put it on-screen."

The huge viewscreen flickered and a man's face appeared.

Oh, wow. Eve blinked. He was clearly Eon, but he was so handsome that it nearly hurt to look at him. He was built like a warrior, broad shoulders stretching a sleeveless, blue shirt, and a cord of gold strained around a muscled bicep. But where Davion's face had a rugged edge, the king's was pure, masculine beauty. He looked like a movie star or model, except one who could also fight a swarm of Kantos, if required.

"War Commander Thann-Eon." A deep, authoritative voice.

"Your majesty." Davion bowed his head.

"Davion, I am very happy to see that you're alive."

"Me too, Gayel."

The easy familiarity made Eve stare at Davion. It was clear they were friends.

"I've been informed of your…ordeal," the king said.

"Yes. The Kantos." Davion launched into a quick recap of events on Hunter7.

The king's gaze moved to Eve and she straightened.

"Gayel, this is Sub-Captain Eve Traynor of Earth. Eve, this is King Gayel Solann-Eon."

"Uh, King Solann-Eon." She bowed her head. Shit, she hoped she wasn't supposed to curtsy or anything.

"I'm not impressed with your planet's decision to abduct my war commander, Sub-Captain Traynor."

She swallowed. "Sorry about that. I thought it was a terrible idea too." She blew out a breath. "But the Kantos are closing in on Earth, and our backs are to the wall. Your people have the ability to help us, but have ignored us for decades."

The king was quiet for a long moment, then looked at Davion. "She is your mate?"

"Yes." Davion smiled down at Eve. "She's my everything."

Looking at him made her nerves melt away. She smiled back, linking her hand with his.

The king made a sound and when Eve looked up, she realized he was laughing.

Shit, for a split second, she'd forgotten all about him.

"Please, your majesty. Earth needs your help. The Kantos are our common enemy, and they won't stop—"

The king held up a hand and she closed her mouth. He opened his mouth to speak in turn, but was interrupted by Davion.

"Sire, I fully back my mate. If the Eon don't agree to help Earth, I will henceforth resign my commission and go back with her."

"What?" Eve stared at him.

All around them, there were indrawn breaths and shocked looks. The king was silent, his expression pensive.

"I will not be separated from you. And I sure as Cren won't leave your sisters and your planet to be destroyed."

God, the man was crazy about her. "I love you," she whispered.

"I love you too." Davion pulled her tightly to his side.

The king cleared his throat. "It is true that my father was stuck in the old ways, and this is something that I have long questioned. If my best war commander has accepted you as his mate, you must be an incredible woman, Eve Traynor. And I hope that means Terrans have qualities that we've thus far underestimated."

"The people of Earth are both good and bad, your

majesty. We're not perfect. Regardless, we deserve to live, and will fight to survive."

"Fierce. And I see you have grit and loyalty. All very good qualities." The king glanced at Davion and smiled. "Well done, War Commander."

Davion's fingers tightened around Eve's.

"Unlike my father, I dislike the idea of leaving an entire species in firing range of the Kantos. We will help Earth."

Relief washed through Eve and she blew out a breath. But then the king's face changed. If he'd been on the bridge, Eve was sure she'd have felt the full force of his anger fill the room.

"Unfortunately, abducting Davion wasn't your planet's only ill-advised decision."

Dread trickled in. "Oh?"

"They've also hijacked the *Desteron's* sister warship, the *Rengard*."

More shocked breaths and a few curses.

"Eon High Command's last contact with the ship said that whomever Earth had sent had infiltrated the ship and taken over the ship's systems."

"All of the ship's systems?" Brack asked incredulously.

"All of them, Second Commander Thann-Felis. War Commander Dann-Jad was tearing the ship apart to find the hijacker when the ship's stardrives ignited, and it disappeared."

Oh, shit. Eve's palms were sweaty again. What the hell had Space Corps done? And who the hell would have been crazy enough or skilled enough to pull this off?

"They also sent another operative who snuck into our sacred temple on Felis. They stole the sacred gem of Ston."

Now Eve felt a rumble of anger from the agitated warriors on the bridge. She squeezed her eyes closed.

"We suspect the thief will be going after the gems of Alqin and Eschar, as well."

Davion gripped her hand hard.

This was *not* good.

DAVION WATCHED EVE'S TENSE, pale face and wanted to hug her.

"Gayel," Davion said. "If we announce a treaty with Earth, I'm sure all of this can be rectified."

Eve nodded. "I can talk to my planet's leaders. They're desperate. Clearly, they didn't just send me to kidnap Davion—" When the king's jaw tightened, she hurried on. "—and they probably expected me to fail."

"So, they sent a thief and a hijacker as insurance, as well," the king said unhappily.

"Ah...sorry."

"Status on the jewels and the *Rengard*?" Davion asked.

"High Command lost contact with the warship in the Syrann Quadrant. There's been no contact since."

Eve groaned and Davion stroked her back. How the hell could someone steal a warship filled with Eon Warriors? He looked down at Eve and fought a smile. Eve could probably do it, if she set her mind to it. He released a breath. War Commander Malax Dann-Jad was a friend, and a very good warrior. The man would be enraged.

"We do have a lead on the jewel thief," the king continued. "I want someone sent after this Terran. To recover the gem of Ston, and to stop them from stealing the other two sacred gems." The king's gaze moved past Davion and settled on Caze. "I was hoping to borrow your security commander, Davion. I believe he has the requisite skills to carry out this mission."

Davion nodded. Caze had spent several years as a stealth operative. And there was no warrior more dedicated when assigned a task.

Caze snapped to attention. "I'll do as ordered, your majesty."

Davion inclined his head. "There is no better warrior for the job."

"We have a partial image of the thief," the king said. "It was taken from the temple security system."

A picture flashed onto the screen and Davion blinked. It was a female.

Eve gasped. "Oh, no."

He turned. "What?"

She grimaced. "I...uh, I know who the thief is."

Davion stared at her. "Go on."

"That's my sister. Lara."

Davion studied the image. It wasn't clear, but he could see the woman did look similar to Eve. He was used to Eon looking alike, and he'd forgotten that looks varied more widely on Earth. But not for the Traynor sisters. Lara Traynor could be Eve's twin, except she looked a little more muscular.

Davion looked at his boots and he heard Gayel make a strangled sound.

"Oh, shit," Eve breathed. "The *Rengard*—"

Davion looked at her. "What about it?"

"No. She wouldn't have..." Eve pressed a palm to her forehead. "My younger sister, Wren. She's a genius with computer systems. If anyone could hijack a warship, it's her." Eve gripped his arm. "But she's not military, Dav. She's not trained."

"It's okay, Eve. We'll sort this out."

Suddenly, anger flooded Eve's face and her hands curled into fists. "Fucking Space Corps. They must have blackmailed my sisters into doing this. The bastards."

"I'll find the thief." Caze's dark tone held an edge.

Eve spun. "You won't hurt her."

Caze's set face didn't change. "I'll do what the mission requires."

Eve took a menacing step forward. "You hurt my sister, warrior, and I'll hurt you."

Davion wrapped an arm around Eve, yanking her back against his chest. "No bloodshed on my bridge, please." He glanced at his warrior. "Please bring my mate's sister to us. Alive and unharmed."

Eve tugged away from Davion, her hot gaze still on Caze. "You know what, Lara will probably hurt *you*."

Caze made a scoffing sound.

"She's a trained special forces space marine." Eve's smile was a little scary. "And she can be mean when she needs to. Watch your back, warrior."

Davion decided it was time to defuse the situation. "Caze, take a shuttle and go. Recover the jewel, and bring Lara Traynor to the *Desteron*."

Caze nodded, gave one last unhappy look at Eve, then strode off the bridge.

The king cleared his throat. "Eve Thann-Eon—"

Eve started. "I beg your pardon? What did you call me?"

"You're mated to Davion. That means you take his clan designation."

She blinked. Davion bit his lip. He hadn't had a chance to talk to her about this.

"I'm appointing you the Terran ambassador to the Eon Empire," the king said.

Eve's eyes bugged out of her head. "You're what? You can't do that. I'm a Space Corps Sub-Captain. No, I'm not even that. I'm a criminal—"

"My decree stands. You will be assigned to the *Desteron*. If we are to beat the Kantos, we need to work together. We need to make this alliance work."

Eve's mouth snapped shut and she nodded.

"I want my warship and sacred gems returned, Ambassador."

"Right," Eve said.

"Davion, congratulations on your mating. When the time is right, I look forward to welcoming you and your mate to my palace on Eon."

"Thank you, your majesty."

The screen went black. Davion swiveled. "Brack, let's begin the search for the *Rengard*. Set course for the Syrann Quadrant."

"On it."

Davion turned to Eve. "Ambassador."

She wrinkled her nose. "Don't call me that."

"When we're in range, I'll set up a secure line to Earth. It's time to save your planet, and your sisters."

"And kick some Kantos ass."

Davion laughed. *By the Alqin's axe*, he loved his bloodthirsty mate.

CHAPTER TWENTY

Lara

Lara Traynor squeezed out of the narrow tunnel and came out on top of the wall. She crouched there, balanced high above the temple forecourt.

The temple was sturdy. It had a masculine feel, with lots of straight lines, blocky towers, and large, regular columns. She liked it a lot. The Eon were good at more than just creating badass warriors and technology.

And here she was, sneaking into another Eon temple. Not exactly how she'd seen her career going, but Lara liked getting her missions done—no matter what.

She swiveled, and pressed her special climbing gloves and boots to the slick rock. She started making her way down the stone wall.

She already had one of the sacred Eon gems in her possession. The gorgeous, seafoam-colored stone, the Ston gem, was hidden on her stealth ship. The amazing jewel actually had a live, alien symbiont inside it. *Incredible.*

Now she was after her second target—the Alqin gem.

As she climbed down the wall, her thoughts turned to her sister.

Was Eve still alive? Heat shot through Lara, leaving a bad taste in her mouth. Fucking Space Corps. They'd fucked her family over so many times, and now they'd sent Eve on a suicide mission. It made Lara want to punch someone in the face. Preferably an admiral or two.

And here she was, blackmailed into this insane mission.

Her boots touched stone, and she turned away from the wall. She crouched down and held her breath, studying the shadowed courtyard and listening for any sound.

Just the tinkle of a water fountain and the faint glow from lights inside. After she had gem number two, she just needed the third and final one, then she was going to find out what the hell had happened to Eve.

She rose, heading toward the statue in the very center of the courtyard. The gem rested on the crown of the god.

"Bad choice, Terran."

The deep voice made her spin. It was cold and dark, and sent shivers up her spine.

She flipped one arm out, her blade dropping from her forearm holder and into her hand. She scanned the darkness but couldn't see him.

Then he stepped out of the shadows.

Holy cow. He was huge. An Eon warrior wearing full, black-scale armor.

He had a raw, masculine face with a hard edge. It looked like it had been carved from granite. And cold eyes.

Their gazes locked, and tension wound between them. His eyes were black as night, with thin threads of silver through them.

At the same time, they launched at each other.

Lara slashed out with her knife. He blocked her blow, and she veered away. Then, he swung a punch at her, and she ducked. She kicked, aiming for his legs, but he jumped, leaping over her leg.

They both spun away, circling each other. She watched as a long, blue sword formed on his arm. Oh, man. She'd heard about the symbiont-formed weapons. Damn thing was gorgeous. She wanted one.

He charged and Lara rushed to meet him.

They traded hits and kicks. She put all her effort into avoiding that glowing sword. The warrior was big, strong, and well-trained, but Lara had been born to fight, and her job had honed her abilities.

She leaped up and kicked. Her boot connected with his strong jaw, and his head snapped back.

Lara smirked. "Like that?"

The warrior growled and swung out with his sword. She dodged, the blade slamming into a pillar.

She lifted her head and laughed. "What was that? A love tap?"

Now, she felt a throb of annoyance and anger off Mr. Cool. They launched into another deadly dance. They passed the pond, and Lara leaped over the water and its lily pads. The warrior followed her.

It didn't take her long to see he wasn't using his full strength against her. That pissed her off.

"You're holding back," she snapped.

"Eve asked me not to hurt you."

Lara stilled. "Eve?" A flood of emotion tightened Lara's throat. "She's alive?"

"Yes." One cool word.

If that was true, then she was a prisoner of the Eon. Could she trust this deadly warrior?

Lara stroked her blade, working through all the scenarios. This changed nothing. She still needed to complete her mission.

Lara quickly snatched a StrikeBolt off her belt. She tossed it through the air.

It made a small whistling sound and the warrior dodged. But he was a shade too slow, and the small device caught his side. Small prongs flared, digging into him.

Blue electricity raced over his body. She saw his jaw lock and he dropped to his knees.

Lara sauntered over and snatched up the gem of Alqin.

"It's been a good time, warrior."

"I'll... Come for you." He pushed the words out through gritted teeth.

Lara had felt the effects of the StrikeBolt in training. She'd passed out within seconds. She'd never seen anyone stay conscious this long.

"You'll...feel my breath... Back of your neck. I'll hunt you to the end of the galaxy."

Lara felt a cold shiver. "You can try."

With the electricity holding him still, she raced across

the courtyard and back to the wall. She braced a hand against the stone and glanced back.

His black-and-silver eyes were locked on her.

She tossed him a salute and started climbing.

Now, she needed to get off this planet and head to the temple on a small moon of Ath. Two gems down, one to go.

She needed to finish her mission, and save Earth and her sisters.

And on top of that, she also now needed to avoid one very angry Eon warrior.

Lara smiled grimly. *Should be child's play.*

EVE STRODE down the corridor of the *Desteron*. Out the window, stars streamed past. It had only been a few days, but God, she loved this ship.

A warrior approached from the opposite direction, wearing *Desteron* black. He wasn't as big as Davion, but there were still plenty of muscles on display. The warrior stopped and stood to the side, snapping to attention, his head bowed.

"Ambassador."

Eve tried hard not to wrinkle her nose. She was still adjusting to the title. Hell, she was still adjusting to everything, and so were the Eon. The warship's warriors were still a little cautious and wary of her.

But every night ended with her wrapped in Davion's arms in their bed. That made it all worthwhile.

"Ambassador."

Brack also entered the hall, nodding at the young warrior.

"I told you to call me Eve," she told Davion's second.

"I know." He shot her a grin. "But I like seeing you wrinkle your nose."

Brack was turning out to be the brother she'd always wished she'd had, and now knew she was grateful she'd missed out on. So damn annoying.

"The war commander sent me to tell you that we've made contact with Earth."

Finally. "Thanks, Brack."

He swiveled and strode off. She inclined her head at the young warrior, who was still standing at attention.

He nodded in return, then hesitated.

"Was there something you needed?" she asked.

"The war commander has praised your fighting abilities. A group of us wondered if you would be interested in running some training sessions for us."

Warmth hit her. "A chance to kick some warrior ass?"

The young warrior blinked. "Sorry?"

Right. Be more serious, Eve. She met the man's gaze. "Of course. I'd love to."

The warrior gave her a faint smile. "Thank you, Ambassador."

As he headed off down the corridor, Eve wrinkled her nose. She turned and made for the lift to take her to Davion's office.

When she reached his domain and the door opened, she took a second to drink him in. God, he looked so gorgeous and proper sitting behind that big desk. She'd been itching for days to get her oh-so-sexy war commander to break that desk in with her. He'd recently showered, and his uniform was neatly pressed and his hair brushed into a neat style.

He looked up and smiled.

Eve circled the black desk and dropped into his lap. She reached up and messed up his hair.

"Hello, War Commander."

"Ambassador."

"Stop calling me that." She kissed him, biting his bottom lip.

"It is your new title. You need to get used to it." He deepened the kiss and she moaned into his mouth.

When he pulled back, she saw heat in his eyes.

She stroked the shiny surface of the desk. "I've had a few fantasies about you, me, and this desk."

His desire pulsed through the air. "I hope to make those a reality for you, however, I have an Admiral Barber holding on the comm line."

Eve squeaked and scrambled off his lap. "Why didn't you tell me that when I first got here?"

"Because you sat in my lap, and I got distracted by my enticing mate."

She shook her head and straightened her shirt. He stood with her, his smile widening. Then they both turned to face the screen on the wall.

It flickered and Admiral Barber's face appeared.

When she saw Eve, relief crossed the woman's face. "Eve. I am so very happy to see you."

"See me alive, you mean."

The admiral smiled, shooting a cautious look at

Davion before she looked at Eve again. "Yes." Then she looked at Davion. "War Commander Thann-Eon."

"Admiral Barber."

Ooh, he was using his scary, badass tone.

"I hope the fact that you're calling and you're alive means your mission was a...success," the admiral said.

Eve snorted. "Not really."

Davion stepped closer. "I do not appreciate being abducted off my own warship, Admiral."

Barber barely controlled a wince. "I am very sorry. Circumstances forced us to make difficult decisions."

"Luckily for you, Eve has convinced me of this."

Hope flared in the admiral's eyes. "The Kantos must be stopped."

"Agreed. My king has agreed to help Earth."

"Thank the stars." The admiral released a shaky breath.

"But there can be no more secret missions against the Eon."

Eve watched Barber's face go from pleased to uncomfortable.

Eve crossed her arms. "Where are my sisters, Admiral?"

Barber released a breath. "Sending your sisters on those missions was not my decision. But they were offered a chance to free you, and they readily agreed."

Eve cursed. Of course, they did. "They were bribed and blackmailed, you mean." *Damn you, Lara and Wren.* She loved her sisters, but they drove her crazy.

"Recall them," Davion said.

"The Eon are not happy," Eve added. "Not with their sacred jewels and warship missing."

The admiral cleared her throat. "They're out of contact."

Eve pressed her lips together. "Dammit."

"I'll do what I can." Barber looked at Davion. "When can you return Eve to Earth?"

"Never."

The admiral looked alarmed. "War Commander, she is not to blame for any of this—"

Eve held up a hand. "The king has named me the Terran ambassador to the Eon Empire."

"Oh. That's excellent news." The admiral sounded giddy. "But I still don't understand why you can't return home."

Davion stepped closer, pressing his front to Eve's back. He wrapped an arm around her. "Because I will not let her go."

Barber frowned, looking confused.

Eve tipped her head back to look at her warrior. "Nothing could convince me to come back to Earth right now."

"And nothing will ever convince me to give her up." Davion lowered his mouth, kissing her.

Eve smiled against his delicious mouth, feeling the wash of his feelings. Such a fierce love.

"You... I..." The admiral sounded shocked.

Eve rubbed her nose against Davion's before she turned back to the screen. She tried to find a diplomatic way to tell the admiral that she'd fallen in love with the alien war commander she'd abducted.

"Eve and I are mated," Davion stated baldly.

Or they could just take the direct approach.

Barber made a choked sound. "You're what?"

"Mated," Eve said. "Hitched. I'm, um, Eve Thann-Eon, now."

"Ambassador Eve Thann-Eon," Davion said.

"I don't know what to say." Barber shook her head. "Congratulations."

"Thanks," Eve said. "Now, we'll be focused on plans to take down the Kantos. And I want you to find my sisters, Admiral."

The other woman nodded.

"Then we will destroy the Kantos," Davion added.

Now Barber smiled. "For the first time, I have hope. Thank you, Eve, War Commander."

As the call disconnected, Davion pulled Eve into his arms.

"You were hard on her," he said.

"She deserved it."

"I'm grateful to her and the Space Corps."

Eve pulled back. "What?"

He nibbled her lips. "She sent you to kidnap me."

"Oh?"

He spun Eve and lifted her onto his desk. A comp tablet fell to the floor and they both ignored it. Heat flared in his eyes. "I'm grateful I found you, my mate."

"Me, too." She started tugging at his uniform.

"I'm grateful that I get to hold you, touch you." He ran his hands down her body. "Even if I have to battle an alien species for you. Actually, I'm very good at battling alien species."

"For now, let's focus on the holding and touching." She bared his hard chest and ran her hands over his skin.

"Mostly, I'm grateful that I get to love you, Eve. And that you love me."

She cupped his cheek. "Me too, warrior. Now, how about we test out this desk of yours, and you show me how much you love me?"

He pushed her back onto the desk. "I am a warrior of action."

Her warrior. No matter what they faced. Eve kissed her mate and pulled him down on top of her.

I hope you enjoyed Eve and Davion's story!

Eon Warriors continues with *Touch of Eon* starring Lieutenant Lara Traynor and Eon warrior Caze. Coming January 8th 2019.

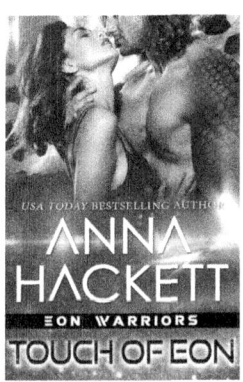

For more action-packed romance, read on for a preview of

the first chapter of *Gladiator,* the first book in my best-selling Galactic Gladiators series.

Don't miss out! For updates about new releases, action romance info, free books, and other fun stuff, sign up for my VIP mailing list and get your *free box set* containing three action-packed romances.

Visit here to get started: www.annahackettbooks.com

JOIN THE ACTION-PACKED ADVENTURE!

PREVIEW: GLADIATOR

MORE SCI-FI ROMANCE

Fighting for love, honor, and freedom on the galaxy's lawless outer rim.

Fighting for love, honor, and freedom on the galaxy's lawless outer rim...

When Earth space marine Harper Adams finds herself abducted by alien slavers off a space station, her life turns into a battle for survival. Dumped into an arena on a desert planet on the outer rim, she finds herself face to face with a big, tattooed alien gladiator...the champion of the Kor Magna Arena.

PREVIEW: GLADIATOR

Just another day at the office.

Harper Adams pulled herself along the outside of the space station module. She could hear her quiet breathing inside her spacesuit, and she easily pulled her weightless body along the slick, white surface of the module. She stopped to check a security panel, ensuring all the systems were running smoothly.

Check. Same as it had been yesterday, and the day before that. But Harper never ever let herself forget that they were six hundred million kilometers away from Earth. That meant they were dependent only on themselves. She tapped some buttons on the security panel before closing the reinforced plastic cover. She liked to dot all her *I*s and cross all her *T*s. She never left anything to chance.

She grabbed the handholds and started pulling herself up over the cylindrical pod to check the panels on the other side. Glancing back behind herself, she caught a beautiful view of the planet below.

Harper stopped and made herself take it all in. The orange, white, and cream bands of Jupiter could take your breath away. Today, she could even see the famous superstorm of the Great Red Spot. She'd been on the Fortuna Research Station for almost eighteen months. That meant, despite the amazing view, she really didn't see it anymore.

She turned her head and looked down the length of the space station. At the end was the giant circular donut that housed the main living quarters and offices. The main ring rotated to provide artificial gravity for the residents. Lying off the center of the ring was the long cylinder of the research facility, and off that cylinder were several modules that housed various scientific labs and storage. At the far end of the station was the docking area for the supply ships that came from Earth every few months.

"Lieutenant Adams? Have you finished those checks?"

Harper heard the calm voice of her fellow space marine and boss, Captain Samantha Santos, through the comm system in her helmet.

"Almost done," Harper answered.

"Take a good look at the botany module. The computer's showing some strange energy spikes, but the scientists in there said everything looks fine. Must be a system malfunction."

Which meant the geek squad engineers were going to have to come in and do some maintenance. "On it."

Harper swung her body around, and went feet-first down the other side of the module. She knew the rest of the security team—all made up of United Nations Space Marines—would be running similar checks on the other modules across the station. They had a great team to ensure the safety of the hundreds of scientists aboard the station. There was also a dedicated team of engineers that kept the guts of the station running.

She passed a large, solid window into the module, and could see various scientists floating around benches filled with all kinds of plants. They all wore matching gray jumpsuits accented with bright-blue at the collars, that indicated science team. There was a vast mix of scientists and disciplines aboard—biologists, botanists, chemists, astronomers, physicists, medical experts, and the list went on. All of them were conducting experiments, and some were searching for alien life beyond the edge of the solar system. It seemed like every other week, more probes were being sent out to hunt for radio signals or collect samples.

Since humans had perfected large solar sails as a way to safely and quickly propel spacecraft, getting around the solar system had become a lot easier. With radiation pressure exerted by sunlight onto the mirrored sails, they could travel from Earth to Fortuna Station orbiting Jupiter in just a few months. And many of the scientists aboard the station were looking beyond the solar system, planning manned expeditions farther and farther away. Harper wasn't sure they were quite ready for that.

She quickly checked the adjacent control panel. Among all the green lights, she spotted one that was blinking red, and she frowned. They definitely had a problem with the locking system on the exterior door at the end of the module. She activated the small propulsion pack on her spacesuit, and circled around the module. She slowed down as she passed the large, round exterior door at the end of the cylindrical module.

It was all locked into place and looked secure.

As she moved back to the module, she grabbed a handhold and then tapped the small tablet attached to the forearm of her suit. She keyed in a request for maintenance to come and check it.

She looked up and realized she was right near

another window. Through the reinforced glass, a pretty, curvy blonde woman looked up and spotted Harper. She smiled and waved. Harper couldn't help but smile and lifted her gloved hand in greeting.

Dr. Regan Forrest was a botanist and a few years younger than Harper. The young woman was so open and friendly, and had befriended Harper from her first day on the station. Harper had never had a lot of friends —mainly because she'd been too busy raising her younger sister and working. She'd never had time for girly nights out or gossip.

But Regan was friendly, smart, and had the heart of a steamroller under her pretty exterior. Harper always had trouble saying no to her. Maybe the woman reminded her a little of Brianna. At the thought of her sister, something twisted painfully in Harper's chest.

Regan floated over to the window and held up a small tablet. She'd typed in some words.

Cards tonight?

Harper had been teaching Regan how to play poker. The woman was terrible at it, and Harper beat her all the time. But Regan never gave up.

Harper nodded and held up two fingers to indicate a couple of hours. She was off-shift shortly, and then she had a sparring match with Regan's cousin, Rory—one of the station engineers—in the gym. Aurora "Call me Rory or I'll hit you" Fraser had been trained in mixed martial arts, and Harper found the female engineer a hell of a sparring partner. Rory was teaching Harper some martial arts moves and Harper was showing the woman some basic sword moves. Since she was little, Harper had been a keen fencer.

Regan grinned back and nodded. Then the woman's wide smile disappeared. She spun around, and through the glass Harper could see the other scientists all looking around, concerned. One scientist was spinning around, green plants floating in the air around him, along with fat droplets of water and some other green fluid. He'd clearly screwed up and let his experiment get free.

"Lieutenant Adams?" The captain's voice came through her helmet again. "Harper?"

There was a sense of urgency that made Harper's belly tighten. "Go ahead, Captain."

"We have an alarm sounding in the botany module. The computer says there is a risk of decompression."

Dammit. "I just checked the security panels. The locking mechanism on the exterior door is showing red. I did a visual inspection and it's closed up tight."

"Okay, we talked with the scientist in charge. Looks like one of her team let something loose in there. It isn't dangerous, but it must be messing with the alarm sensors. System's locked them all in there." She made an annoyed sound. "Idiots will have to stay there until engineering can get down there and free them."

Harper studied the room through the glass again. Some of the green liquid had floated over to another bench that contained various frothing cylinders on it. A second later, the cylinders shattered, their contents bubbling upward.

The scientists all moved to the back exit of the

module, banging on the locked door. *Damn*. They were trapped.

Harper met Regan's gaze. Her friend's face was pale, and wisps of her blonde hair had escaped her ponytail, floating around her face.

"Captain," Harper said. "Something's wrong. The experiments have overflowed their containment." She could see the scientists were all coughing.

"Engineering is on the way," the captain said.

Harper pushed herself off, flying over the surface of the module. She reached the control panel and saw that several other lights had turned red. They needed to get this under control and they needed to do it now.

"Harper!" The captain's panicked voice. "Decompression in progress!"

What the hell? The module jerked beneath Harper. She looked up and saw the exterior door blow off, flying away from the station.

Her heart stopped. That meant all the scientists were exposed to the vacuum of space.

Fuck. Harper pushed off again, sending herself flying toward the end of the module. She put her arms by her sides to help increase her speed. Through the window, she saw that most of the scientists had grabbed on to whatever they could hold on to. A few were pulling emergency breathers over their heads.

She reached the end of the pod and saw the damage. There was torn metal where the door had been ripped off. Inside the door, she knew there would be a temporary repair kit containing a sheet of high-tech nano fabric that could be stretched across the opening to reestablish pressure. But it needed to be put in place manually. Harper reached for the latch to release the repair kit.

Suddenly, a slim body shot out of the pod, her arms and legs kicking. Her mouth was wide open in a silent scream.

Regan. Harper didn't let herself think. She turned, pushed off and fired her propulsion system, arrowing after her friend.

"Security Team to the botany module," she yelled through her comm system. "Security Team to botany module. We have decompression. One scientist has been expelled. I'm going after her. I need someone that can help calm the others and get the module sealed again."

"Acknowledged, Lieutenant," Captain Santos answered. "I'm on my way."

Harper focused on reaching Regan. She was gaining on her. She saw that the woman had lost consciousness. She also knew that Regan had only a couple of minutes to survive out here. Harper let her training take over. She tapped the propulsion system controls, trying for more speed, as she maneuvered her way toward Regan.

As she got close, Harper reached out and wrapped her arm around the scientist. "I've got you."

Harper turned, at the same time clipping a safety line to the loops on Regan's jumpsuit. Then, she touched the controls and propelled them straight back towards the module. She kept her friend pulled tightly toward her chest. *Hold on, Regan.*

She was so still. It reminded Harper of holding Brianna's dead body in her arms. Harper's jaw tightened. She wouldn't let Regan die out here. The woman had dreamed of working in space, and worked her entire career to get here, even defying her family. Harper wasn't going to fail her.

As the module got closer, she saw that the security team had arrived. She saw the captain's long, muscled body as she and another man put up the nano fabric.

"Incoming. Keep the door open."

"Can't keep it open much longer, Adams," the captain replied. "Make it snappy."

Harper adjusted her course, and, a second later, she shot through the door with Regan in her arms. Behind her, the captain and another huge security marine, Lieutenant Blaine Strong, pulled the stretchy fabric across the opening.

"Decompression contained," the computer intoned.

Harper released a breath. On the panel beside the door, she saw the lights turning green. The nano fabric wouldn't hold forever, but it would do until they got everyone out of here, and then got a maintenance team in here to fix the door.

"Oxygen levels at required levels," the computer said again.

"Good work, Lieutenant." Captain Sam Santos floated over. She was a tall woman with a strong face and brown hair she kept pulled back in a tight ponytail. She had curves she kept ruthlessly toned, and golden skin she always said was thanks to her Puerto Rican heritage.

"Thanks, Captain." Harper ripped her helmet off and looked down at Regan.

Her blonde hair was a wild tangle, her face was pale and marked by what everyone who worked in space called space hickeys—bruises caused by the skin's small blood vessels bursting when exposed to the vacuum of space. *Please be okay.*

"Here." Blaine appeared, holding a portable breather. The big man was an excellent marine. He was about six foot five with broad shoulders that stretched his spacesuit to the limit. She knew he was a few inches over the height limit for space operations, but he was a damn good marine, which must have gone in his favor. He had dark skin thanks to his African-American father and his handsome face made him popular with the station's single ladies, but mostly he worked and hung out with the other marines.

"Thanks." Harper slipped the clear mask over Regan's mouth.

"Nice work out there." Blaine patted her shoulder. "She's alive because of you."

Suddenly, Regan jerked, pulling in a hard breath.

"You're okay." Harper gripped Regan's shoulder. "Take it easy."

Regan looked around the module, dazed and panicky. Harper watched as Regan caught sight of the fabric stretched across the end of the module, and all the plants floating around inside.

"God," Regan said with a raspy gasp, her breath fogging up the dome of the breather. She shook her head, her gaze moving to Harper. "Thanks, Harper."

"Any time." Harper squeezed her friend's shoulder. "It's what I'm here for."

Regan managed a wan smile. "No, it's just you. You

didn't have to fly out into space to rescue me. I'm grateful."

"Come on. We need to get you to the infirmary so they can check you out. Maybe put some cream on your hickeys."

"Hickeys?" Regan touched her face and groaned. "Oh, no. I'm going to get a ribbing."

"And you didn't even get them the pleasurable way."

A faint blush touched Regan's cheeks. "That's right. If I had, at least the ribbing would have been worth it."

With a relieved laugh, Harper looked over at her captain. "I'm going to get Regan to the infirmary."

The other woman nodded. "Good. We'll meet you back at the Security Center."

With a nod, Harper pushed off, keeping one arm around Regan, and they floated into the main part of the science facility. Soon, they moved through the entrance into the central hub of the space station. As the artificial gravity hit, Harper's boots thudded onto the floor. Beside her, Regan almost collapsed.

Harper took most of the woman's weight and helped her down the corridor. They pushed into the infirmary.

A gray-haired, barrel-chested man rushed over. "Decided to take an unscheduled spacewalk, Dr. Forrest?"

Regan smiled weakly. "Yes. Without a spacesuit."

The doctor made a tsking sound and then took her from Harper. "We'll get her all patched up."

Harper nodded. "I'll come and check on you later."

Regan grabbed her hand. "We have a blackjack game

scheduled. I'm planning to win back all those chocolates you won off me."

Harper snorted. "You can try." It was good to see some life back in Regan's blue eyes.

As Harper strode out into the corridor, she ran a hand through her dark hair, tension slowly melting out of her shoulders. She really needed a beer. She tilted her neck one way and then the other, hearing the bones pop.

Just another day at the office. The image of Regan drifting away from the space station burst in her head. Harper released a breath. She was okay. Regan was safe and alive. That was all that mattered.

With a shake of her head, Harper headed toward the Security Center. She needed to debrief with the captain and clock off. Then she could get out of her spacesuit and take the one-minute shower that they were all allotted.

That was the one thing she missed about Earth. Long, hot showers.

And swimming. She'd been a swimmer all her life and there were days she missed slicing through the water.

She walked along a long corridor, meeting a few people—mainly scientists. She reached a spot where there was a long bank of windows that afforded a lovely view of Jupiter, and space beyond it.

Stingy showers and unscheduled spacewalks aside, Harper had zero regrets about coming out into space. There'd been nothing left for her on Earth, and to her surprise, she'd made friends here on Fortuna.

As she stared out into the black, mesmerized by the twinkle of stars, she caught a small flash of light in the distance. She paused, frowning. What the hell was that?

She stared hard at the spot where she'd seen the flash. Nothing there but the pretty sprinkle of stars. Harper shook her head. Fatigue was playing tricks on her. It had to have just been a weird trick of the lights reflecting off the glass.

Pushing the strange sighting away, she continued on to the Security Center.

Galactic Gladiators
Gladiator
Warrior
Hero
Protector
Champion
Barbarian
Beast
Rogue
Guardian
Cyborg
Also Available as Audiobooks!

PREVIEW - HELL SQUAD: MARCUS

READY FOR ANOTHER?

IN THE AFTERMATH OF AN ALIEN INVASION:

**HEROES WILL RISE...
WHEN THEY HAVE
SOMEONE TO LIVE FOR**

In the aftermath of a deadly alien invasion, a band of survivors fights on...

In a world gone to hell, Elle Milton—once the darling of the Sydney social scene—has carved a role for herself as the communications officer for the toughest commando team fighting for humanity's survival—Hell Squad. It's her chance to make a difference and make up for horrible past mistakes...despite the fact that its battle-hardened commander never wanted her on his team.

When Hell Squad is tasked with destroying a strategic alien facility, Elle knows they need her skills in the field. But first she must go head to head with Marcus Steele and convince him she won't be a liability.

Marcus Steele is a warrior through and through. He fights to protect the innocent and give the human race a chance to survive. And that includes the beautiful, gutsy Elle who twists him up inside with a single look. The last thing he wants is to take her into a warzone, but soon they are thrown together battling both the alien invaders and their overwhelming attraction. And Marcus will learn just how much he'll sacrifice to keep her safe.

Hell Squad
Marcus
Cruz
Gabe
Reed
Roth
Noah
Shaw
Holmes
Niko
Finn
Theron
Hemi
Ash
Levi

Manu
Also Available as Audiobooks!

ALSO BY ANNA HACKETT

Team 52

Mission: Her Protection

Mission: Her Rescue

Mission: Her Security

Also Available as Audiobooks!

Treasure Hunter Security

Undiscovered

Uncharted

Unexplored

Unfathomed

Untraveled

Unmapped

Unidentified

Undetected

Also Available as Audiobooks!

Eon Warriors

Edge of Eon

Galactic Gladiators

Gladiator

Warrior

Hero

Protector

Champion

Barbarian

Beast

Rogue

Guardian

Cyborg

Imperator

Also Available as Audiobooks!

Hell Squad

Marcus

Cruz

Gabe

Reed

Roth

Noah

Shaw

Holmes

Niko

Finn

Theron

Hemi

Ash

Levi

Manu

Also Available as Audiobooks!

The Anomaly Series

Time Thief

Mind Raider

Soul Stealer

Salvation

Anomaly Series Box Set

The Phoenix Adventures

Among Galactic Ruins

At Star's End

In the Devil's Nebula

On a Rogue Planet

Beneath a Trojan Moon

Beyond Galaxy's Edge

On a Cyborg Planet

Return to Dark Earth

On a Barbarian World

Lost in Barbarian Space

Through Uncharted Space

Crashed on an Ice World

Perma Series
Winter Fusion

A Galactic Holiday

Warriors of the Wind
Tempest

Storm & Seduction

Fury & Darkness

Standalone Titles
Savage Dragon

Hunter's Surrender

One Night with the Wolf

For more information visit AnnaHackettBooks.com

ABOUT THE AUTHOR

I'm a USA Today bestselling author and I'm passionate about ***action romance***. I love stories that combine the thrill of falling in love with the excitement of action, danger and adventure. I'm a sucker for that moment when the team is walking in slow motion, shoulder-to-shoulder heading off into battle. I write about people overcoming unbeatable odds and achieving seemingly impossible goals. I like to believe it's possible for all of us to do the same.

My books are mixture of action, adventure and sexy romance and they're recommended for anyone who enjoys fast-paced stories where the boy wins the girl at the end (or sometimes the girl wins the boy!)

For release dates, action romance info, free books, and other fun stuff, sign up for the latest news here:

Website: www.annahackettbooks.com

Printed in Great Britain
by Amazon